Madonna On Her Back

Stories by

Alyson Carol Hagy

Drawings by Lisa Wilkinson

Stuart Wright, Publisher

FIRST EDITION

ISBN: 0-913773-19-0

Library of Congress Catalog Card Number: 86-050089

Author's Acknowledgements

I would first like to note that an early version of this manuscript received the Avery and Jule Hopwood Award for Short Fiction from the University of Michigan in 1984.

I would also like to express my sincere appreciation to the editors of the publications in which the following stories first appeared: *Sewanee Review*, "No Kind of Name"; *Michigan Quarterly Review*, "Stadia"; *Virginia Quarterly Review*, "Where Men Go to Cry"; *Crescent Review*, "Mister Makes" and "Where Men Go to Cry"; and *North American Review*, "Madonna on Her Back."

Most importantly, I wish to deliver my heartfelt thanks to Alan Cheuse, Janet Kauffman, Craig Mueller, Kim Kafka, Janet Hackel, David Rubin, Sheila McMillen, Mandy Pierson, Amy Breakell, and Lisa Wilkinson. And my deepest gratitude and thanks to George Garrett, who filled my small sails with hope, laughter, wisdom, and all the beauty that a story can be.

Tandem Farm
Charlottesville, Virginia

For R.W.S.

Contents

Madonna On Her Back

No Kind of Name

The first yellow squash under her hand was named Judith. The second was Cora; the third was Jane Reid. And today, while starlings knotted the branches of the crab apple trees along the road, the whole apronfull thumping and rolling against her thighs was a Rebecca. Emma shaped and named as the colors and thoughts came to her, falling into her swift fingers. She emptied her apron, carefully pressing her yellow babes together in a crisp bushel basket. She threw a loose and rotting melon—calling it Nina for a moment—into the field to break open in a sweet, fly-breeding stink. An early tomato, soft in her large palm, left its garden vine to be her Rachel, her only. Thinking that its tight skin was likely at any moment, to split and bruise, she placed it gently among the beckoning necks of the squash.

She spoke aloud only as she finished her last row of beans. "You like making me damn tired, don't you?" she said, filling tin pails and an old net-woven onion sack. "Nearly forty years old and you like wasting me away. Year after year." At the sound of her voice, the starlings skittered to higher perches and the stray cat that was hunting in the ditch below the garden slipped into the honeysuckle. But the beans only lay still in thrown bunches waiting for Emma to gather, wash, and give them all away. Anna, Laura, a Rachel, an only—thrown and tossed and moved into crates for market. None of it, none of them, ever came back to her. None of them, as she knew, ever grew again.

Today was a day to do them proud, though. Today, her heart fired in a hard kiln of readiness, Emma had a half bushel of new flat beans for Elias. Elias had taken B. J. Donner's place as the market pick-up man eight, nine weeks ago, and Emma didn't care for him one bit. He stared. He didn't have much to say even though they'd lived on the same road for years. And there was something too well-figured in the way he spit his tobacco. Emma knew he'd be a little bit testy about her beans as he was always coming up her driveway grinning about his quick crops. He didn't have hardly a single, long flat bean yet that she knew of, and hers were just diving from among their leaves like swallows, like mating swallows, she thought. Oh, his green onions and leaf lettuce had come first this spring—he'd left her a mess of both in small paper sacks. But she had him on the beans. And her sweet corn. Jacqueline, Marlene. Her corn was throat high and braiding its tassels up and out into the shimmering sun. On the back of her tongue she was already savoring the look on Elias's dark-skinned face. She knew how it would be. Her tomatoes would seem fuller, her squash would shudder and look brighter to her as he loaded them into the back of his truck. Silently, a laugh would heat her breath as he toed gravel and dragged his lips into a polite smile.

Hooking her fingers under the wire handles of the squash basket, Emma lifted her produce to the level of her waist. Elias was due at nine, and she wanted to have everything clean and some coffee brewed by then. Striding toward the tool shed, she imagined his profile shifting among the squash jostled by her walk. She could see it among the yellow curves—the thin nose, bone firm chin. He was a dark little man, a squeezed-in man who didn't know a goddamn thing about things past his face, the way she saw it. And Lord knows, she told herself as she set the basket on the cool concrete floor of the shed, she ought to be able to have him in for coffee and set a true thing before him.

On Wednesdays at nine a.m., Saturdays at six-thirty, Elias came to take her harvest to the market in town where his cousins Iola and Frank sold it from beneath a sagging tarpaulin—their hands lifting and turning, weighing her produce like it was their own. Emma had been alone and had farmed alone for five summers, digging and planting for her own sake since her father's death and her brother's move to Norfolk and the shipyards. She had no farm hands, no cattle, no pets that she would acknowledge, and she so rarely went any closer to town than

Jones's Grocery and Dairy Products that her neighbors liked to imagine that she really never left her land. It was said that she had taken the farm upon her back, lifting it from her father's crippled hands until her own body and bones bent into a plowshare, a human angle hardened to make something out of nothing. And it was said that the one hundred and eighty acres would suck all of the woman right out of her, that they would leave her dry and cracking next to the rows of dry and cracking work boots abandoned by her father and brother—boots with hollow curls of mud still clasped around the heels.

But Emma, herself, liked to think that she was only doing justice to what she had been given. She—Emma, Emma—was not changed or changeable. In her mind, she snapped her beans in the shade regardless of the seed bills or the rage of thistle in the northern alfalfa field. Sitting spread-kneed on a low three-legged stool, she considered how to call for her elm tree today. Naomi, Brenda, or Rosalie. To her, sorting the stream of names was like pruning, weeding, looking to reap. Letter by letter by name, as her fingers stripped the beans of their tangled ends, she brought life right back into her lap. She crossed her days, with her eyes out upon the land, child by imagined child, planning to do more than stay even like her father had. She snapped and cleaned in an inherited rhythm, but oh, she had to think, the land and the warm fingers of the sun would someday give her more.

The beans were in a beautiful green mound, covered with cotton cloth to keep them from the flies, when Elias swung his rusted Ford pick-up into Emma's driveway. Watching him come toward her, Emma planned how she would save the winning, bragging beans until last. A cup of coffee. An offer of toast or muffins before she showed him. He was early, and there was plenty of time, forty-five minutes or so, for her to uncover her prize and leave him to his regret.

"Morning, Miss Emma," he said as he turned off the ignition, his hat brim slanted over his eyes.

"Morning, Elias."

"You got everything set ready, I see," he said, dropping from the driver's seat to the gravel in one long motion. He hitched his blue work pants up tighter on his narrow hips, and there it was again—the feeling that he was too well-figured, that he had all of his movements in hand. Emma stayed quiet, staring over him into the empty truck bed. "Need any help?" he asked.

"No. I got squash, tomatoes, and the rest ready for you even if you are damn early." She spoke to him, as she always meant to, with her tanned and bare forearms across her chest and her chin held higher than his forehead. Her feet, hot in her leather work shoes, dug into the soft soil beneath the elm.

"Had to get to Fiddler's early," he said, splitting a tight grin that showed his wet, white teeth. "His baby's sick again. Knew you'd be ready anyway."

Emma sighed, her gray eyes as firm as air-dried oak to his face. "It don't make the biggest difference," she said, turning toward the kitchen door as if she'd heard a sound from inside. "Not if that baby's sick. You can bide your time with some coffee if you want."

Elias nodded and took his hat off, smoothing his short, black hair with the side of a forefinger. "Sure," he said, following Emma across the back porch. "I'll be glad to take a little something."

"Just as long as you remember," Emma said, unlatching the screen for the two of them, "to scrape your boots on this outside mat here before you pass through my door."

After the first moment, Emma cursed herself for bringing Elias inside. The storeroom, the hallway, the kitchen all smelled like the freshly-ground coffee she brewed in the morning. The air was sweet and thick among the heavy homemade tables and chairs, and as Elias stood near the window sills lined with ripening tomatoes, Emma realized that she had been wrong to break her rule. Setting each fruit in a separate space, turning each one to face the steady southern sun, she had always told herself that nobody ever had to see what her father and brother hadn't left her. Nobody needed to know that her mother's quilts and recipes weren't enough. But now a man was closed in with her, he was as close as the air. And his nose was wrinkling in the warmth as his hand reached to pull her daddy's very own chair back from the table. She could feel him looking at her, feel him wondering why any woman as ornery as she made herself out to be fixed her life all neat and colorful with bowls of fruits and vegetables scattered on her enameled shelves and knife-knicked counters. She had seen his mama on occasion. She knew that the women in Elias's life barely washed and dried their produce before they grimly stuffed it, boiling, into cans. Probably not a single woman he knew ever looked at what she was doing during those long hours over the steaming sink. Not like he must be looking at her. With his eyes half shut and moving.

She kept her back to him while she poured coffee and lifted muffins from a gold shellacked tin. She tried not to hear the brushing of his pants legs as he sat and shifted. She tried not to smell the clarity of his bleached cotton shirt. She stood with her spine stiff and tightly held until it occurred to her that he would like that, he would like seeing her anchored straight between her hands. He could see the rounding of her hips and buttocks below the pinch of her apron then. He could concentrate on her. And when she heard what she thought was a laugh muffled against his even teeth, she knew it had happened. He had started to think on her in the privacy of her own home. She turned from the counter with a plate in one hand and a muffin in the other. Her hard gray eyes were focused high, as high as the dented pewter plates hanging above the upper shelves. She refused to look lower than the tangled crown of his bare, black-haired head.

After she served Elias his coffee and muffin, Emma turned back toward the windows and counters that were cool with her children. Marguerite, Sara Beth, Leanora. They all ripened beautifully alone. Caroline and Patrice. Their cheeks pressing the window glass, their skins nearly smiling in the light. She could touch them. They moved. They came and went, came and went while Elias sat still in her kitchen, swallowing in gulps. Yes, she'd have to get him behind her, away from her. So far away that he would always look like a speck, a blue-clad speck resting on the horizon. From that distance, she would just be able to see him wave his arms in greeting or anger. She would just be able to hear the notes of his shouts. But she would never be able to tell how he was really feeling. Never make out what he or anyone else might really be saying.

She was imagining the blurred swing of his far-away limbs when she heard him—the real life large-as-her Elias—stand and scuff his boots on her new-polished floor. His words roared, up close, into her ears. "You'll take these for the hospitality, won't you, Miss Emma? I meant to bring them by yesterday." After the roar, there were sounds like he was maybe pulling a crumpled bag from his deepest jacket pocket, like he was holding something in his busy, oil-marked hands. "You're welcome to them," he said.

If he hadn't poured them—green, slim, and strong—onto her kitchen table just as she was turning, shifting, wheeling to cut him off, Emma knew that her heart wouldn't have jumped so. But he dumped them one by one, into the thick air that hung between them. She heard them roll onto the table with the rhythm of her pulse. She saw them settle to lie piled as a gift. Tanya. Katrine. Dahlia. Elias's dark, wide hand played among them as they fell.

"What you got there? What you call them?" she asked in a whisper, her turning caught in her throat.

"Just flat beans. Regular like."

"More than that?" she asked, stepping toward the table to look at the gift that spoke to her with a long list of lives. Nancy and Christine. She hadn't been given anything in seasons and seasons. Ruth and Hannah. Emma reached in and ran her fingers through the beans that, cleaned and strung, looked just like her own. She ran her fingers along them, stroking their fresh crispness absently, stirring around the surface of Elias's wrist as she moved.

"They are beautiful."

"I guess so," Elias said, and she watched him draw his hand back and press it solidly against the covered metal of the tobacco tin he kept in his shirt pocket. She felt like she had never moved so slowly, and she knew no one had ever seen her eyes like they must be, like the deep eyes of a quick-weaned calf. "There's only a half mess or so here," he said. "They won't be weighing in real heavy until next week."

"I like these good enough," she said, leaning in and looking at him from across the walnut table top. "I hope to have some of my own before long. But you're so early." She paused to wet her lips. "Where you ought to be, I guess."

"Ma'am?"

To her, his voice was as steady as her daddy's had ever been. She focused on the shrugging of his neck muscles.

"The summer's peaking, Elias," she said, pushing deep into the beans with her left hand, grabbing one between her fingers and bending it slowly, almost to a snap. "The evenings are long, and I got a fence that needs laying out and putting up."

"Ma'am?"

"I need help. Help, Elias. I'll pay you. In money, in hay bales. Whatever."

Without a second thought, Emma cooked the beans with ham and ate them that day for lunch. Once Elias had left with a promise to redirect the west pasture line and a handwritten order for the hardware store, the coming of the beans had faded. Emma, counting the crab apples—Louisa, Amelia, Fern—in noonlight, was quick to figure what had thrown her. A man in the house. The sounds, the breeze of smells that reminded her too much of her daddy and her brother Martin. But she was sure that she knew how to take care of him. She'd fix a long look on the man, pin him down, name him. Elias, Elias. He had no eyes in the back of his head to see her looking into him. She guessed he really didn't see very much being nearly forty and still at home lining his mama's poplar shelves with applesauce and jelly, fixing his daddy's rust-cut corrugated metal roofs. It didn't matter that the low heat of his eyes and the shiver of his voice were fooling with her for the time being. She'd have him all picked and packaged in a few days.

So Emma watched Elias closely over the next week. She found herself wanting to know what was beneath his hat, his shirt, the heavy shading of his black eyebrows. He was a small man—all shoulders, turns of a closely-cropped head, and hidden legs to her. But she got it in her mind after she drove the wagon of locust posts into the field and Elias lay them, one by one, along the line of the new fence—she got it in her mind that his body, working in rustles, swayed all of his secrets from hip to hip, swinging them from his joints right along the pull of his smile. So she watched him intently as the sun fell and the hot buzz of insects cooled with the dew. Often she sat on the tractor or leaned against the flatbed wagon running her gloved hands along her high, distinct hairline as he worked. Sometimes she paced the even distance between post holes in her boots until it was time to offer Elias ice water from her Thermos or a tomato sandwich from her pocket. But she never invited him in for dinner though he stayed after nine on both Thursday and Friday. She kept her distance, saying little and always remembering that she had housework, pressing housework, that could just as well come first.

Emma was not about to let Elias fool her again. She knew that he was only helping her so that he could get out from under his daddy's failing eyes. It never occurred to her that he hadn't bothered to tell the old man what he was doing in the blue evening light, that the lips of Elias's parents were once again whispering about Bett Tyler and her fatherless children in his absence. She just fed him and made it clear that she didn't mind if he chewed tobacco and spit it every which way. She just worked the tractor with a meanness that flared her nostrils and let him know that, if he was smart, he would allow her to lend a sharp eye to the plotting of the fence. She had pegged him early on as a man who liked to lay his fences slowly, carefully. She had her eyes open. Watching him take off his shirt, even as the heat rose into the night, she could see him sight his line along the reach of his raised arm, marking the boundary from his shoulder to his thumb to the trail of tough, pale posts that grayed out in blurs as they shrank away from him out across the field. Emma watched him plot his line as if it, like the cattle fences out west, might never end. She felt him tell himself, as he planted and steadied every single post, that a real good fence might never be distinguished from the land.

By Saturday, Elias had laid the whole line and both new gateways. It was easy for Emma to tell that he didn't want her help stringing the barbed wire. She saw how his eyes followed the flow of her loose skirts and apron when she got close to where he was working. Once, when the wire popped loose and pulled wild, he asked her to step back, to please step back. "Don't you worry about me," she said to him. "I ain't about to get snagged or wrapped up in anything." But she did move herself away to sit on the empty flatbed that was still attached to the tractor. For the rest of the day she mostly stayed behind him, making the kinds of sounds with her swinging shoes or gloved hands that snapped along the ridges of the farm and came cracking back toward the two of them with the echo of pine or sod. Twice she crossed the creek to check her garden, toeing the potato hills—Dreama, Yvette—and pinching dill heads while she strung songs together in her head. Watching Elias lead the icy clean wire from its rolls, hand over hand, Emma was sure she saw him tilt his ear into the wind as she hummed gospel tunes or fragments of old nursery rhymes to herself. She bit her lips and closed her throat in response.

On Sunday, it was hot and the horizon was still leaking light above the hills when Emma, who was looking over the garden again, ran a stray cat out of the potato patch. Right away, before she had even straightened her back, she hissed at the animal, her hands clapping against her thighs. Right away, she wanted to spit the creature out of her territory, across the creek and toward the road. But while the cat—a gray, thread-striped tabby—leapt away from Emma, covering the creek in a bound, it had no mind to leave the farm. When Emma got back to the fence line where Elias was stapling the top strand of wire onto the posts nearest the first gate, she saw the cat, its eyes carelessly flat in the dusk. It was crouched on Elias's discarded work shirt, kneading the worn blue cotton with its paws, and the man, as Emma could see, didn't care. Elias, his naked back as flat and washed out as the fading locust posts, made no move to chase the animal on. He merely leaned with the leverage of the adjusted wire-stretcher, pulling, breathing heavily over the squeaking strand. She couldn't understand it. The man, Elias, seemed to have the wrong sense of living.

"That cat, Elias, has been in my garden. And I've seen it there before."

"Won't do it no harm," he said, stretching the barbed metal as tight as she could bear to hear it. "They don't eat potatoes or squash."

"They are nuisances. I won't have them and can hardly believe that you let one roll on your shirt like that."

"Shirt's dirty anyway. And besides, she's earned-out tired. Take a look. Ready to drop a litter any moment."

Walking through the gateway and smelling Elias's sweat in the air, Emma worked herself near enough the cat to see that he was right. Though the starved angles of its shoulderblades and spine shadowed its fur, its low hanging belly was tight and full. Its eyes shifted wildly as Emma got close, but it moved nothing more than the twitching curl of its tail. Emma was sure she heard the soft sputter of purring over her own angry breathing.

"Hsst," she said, leaning over the animal. "Hsst. Hssst." But Elias wouldn't have any of it.

"If you'll leave Tabby alone for five minutes, I'll take care of her."

"Tabby?" In her irritation, Emma heard Elias's voice as though it were skidding through a culvert.

"Um-huh. Tabby, Tiger. All the striped ones get that name at my place. And I'll take this one right over there if you dislike her so God-blessed much."

"Tabby. Tiger." Emma turned to look out over the creek where the water still rippled with the last throw of the sun. Dana, Helene. The silhouette of her garden was ragged and still against the sky. "Tabby is no kind of name."

"Look," Elias said, dropping the stapler into the grass at his feet. "I don't much care. A cat don't need that kind of attention. She needs food and a warm corner somewhere." He pulled his gloves off and stuffed them into his back pocket. Reaching for his shirt, he rolled the cat on its back with his hand, rubbing her stretched belly with loose, relaxed fingers. From where she was standing, Emma saw the cat's nipples—swollen, hard, pink with tingling—as eyes or cold round seeds. Elias's fingertips covered them with motion. "Three babies," he said. "Maybe four. I can feel them fairly well." The cat stretched and coiled under his hand. "Come here. Learn something and feel for yourself."

Drawn by the bow of his shoulders which shifted like a white yoke on water as he moved above the darkening grass, Emma knelt by Elias and hung one of her hands in the open air. He took it, guiding it with his dry palm and calloused thumb.

"Just press here. And here," he said, curving her fingers into the pocket of flesh above the cat's thigh. "You can feel them lined up. One, two, three."

Callie, Fiona, Colette. She could feel them bunched and folded in their mother's belly like her own hand bones were folded beneath Elias's. The skin of her arm prickled when she felt his breath. Jeanne, Marie. When she looked up, she was sure she felt the hard brush of his eyes along her throat, her jawline.

She stood too quickly, leaving him before she could even think about the new rush of blood in her forearms. Her plaid cotton skirt whipped toward his face, the scent of soap and mulch on its hem. She tried to think only of one thing. Not the cat, the babies, his shirt, his breath. Just the old hand-made reed-bottomed basket, the brown one, the one she used for weeding.

Emma did not want to hear the sounds Elias made as he crossed the creek behind her. Abigail, Faye. She needed more than anything to feel the tendrils and sagging blossoms of her plants around her ankles. But she heard him just the same. Thick soles crushing the weeds along the creek bank, the scrape of loose pebbles. The sounds pounded with her, in her heart. They chased her right into the furrows of the land.

"Miss Emma, I got something to say." His voice was deep, as deep as the skyline.

Emma broke in. "I'll pay you in cash or with a check either one."

"Why don't you wait a minute," he said. "I ain't asking for my money."

"I'm just going after something," she said, stopping at the edge of the sweet corn, her sweet corn—Evelyn, Darlene—that grew soundlessly in the dark.

"I think we got something right here, Miss Emma. Emma," he said.

"Just let me get a basket for the damned cat. There ain't nothing else."

"Don't you say that to me," he said, moving closer, his pant legs rustling like leaves and vines. "You been watching me for days. Don't say to me that there's nothing to that."

Emma took a step back. Stalks and tassels whispered behind her. Tara, Maureen. "I ain't been looking at nothing special," she said.

"Damn you haven't," he said, moving in, his bare ribs spreading like stems from a cabbage heart as his lungs filled. "I know what you've been thinking about."

"Nothing," she said, her arms close as pods across her chest.

"Just your attraction," he said.

"Nothing."

"Just your loneliness."

"It's nothing you'd understand," she said.

"You been thinking about our being here," he said, meeting and pressing her shoulder with a hard hand until she was backed right into the corn patch.

"Oh, no," she said. Sheila, Linda, Lynn. It wasn't right. Andrea, JoAnn. "This ain't it."

"Ain't what?" he said before he braced her with his hips and one arm sharp in the curve of her spine, before he kissed her.

Lise, Lyda, Lilly, Lillian. The names were taken and spun from between her lips and teeth. And there was nothing else there, nothing beyond the dampness and the heat.

"This ain't love," she said, freeing her mouth and choking to the sky.

"This ain't?" he said, grabbing her, bending and training her backbone backward until the two of them were balanced on the angle of the earth and the air around them whined and cracked with the breaking of cornstalks and the splitting of green cobs.

"What do you call it then?" he shouted as they fell. "What do you call it?"

Mister Makes

"Don't neither of us know what it's like to have a baby with no arms."

"Never want it that way. Thank you, Lord."

"Do you reckon it hurt her much?"

"Surely. Any mama would be hurt by that. Even that one."

"I mean, do you think it hurt coming out?"

"No. Easy birth is what I hear. Probably popped right out. No real shoulders or anything to squeeze through."

"Right after his head came out, you think it was done?"

"Sure. Like any other baby. Like my last three."

"And you don't think it hurt her to have it. She didn't have no idea what was coming?"

"It's not what I hear. I hear she just groaned when they told her, and I don't hear about any bones sticking her or anything."

"Could that happen? Could there be loose ones in there?"

"Sure. Like those calves delivering dead in pieces. Sure it could happen."

"Poor thing. He won't be able to walk or run."

"Why not? He ain't missing his legs."

"She won't be able to get him to crawl or pull himself up on his feet. He won't have balance."

"I ain't saying it'll be easy. But I've seen some—crippled like he is—moving around fine. It ain't like he's blind."

"Well, I'm just saying it'll take years."

"Maybe. Maybe we won't see him do nothing but sit in his yard and moan."

"For four or five years, I say. At least."

"You're thinking she'll stay here?"

"Don't you think so, Mallie? She ain't got nothing but that house."

"You reckon she'll paint the house this time like she did when the first one came home?"

"Don't know. This ain't such a good time. But then the first little one died anyway, didn't it?"

"Sure. Right on the porch one day about two years ago. I saw her crying over it in the middle of them paint buckets."

Leah stared at the venetian blind that they had dropped in her face. Her hand moved up and down, up and down the looped drawstring the nurse had left swinging in the shadows. They were cleaning her bed again. She fingered the frayed brown knots tightened by other patients, hanging onto the grimy string, yanking on it while she kept her back to both nurses.

"You ain't really gonna make me go back to bed, are you? I ain't done nothing. I ain't even seen nothing but a little light from this window. I don't need to be keeping myself in bed when I don't feel like lying down. Nothing wrong with me. I ain't the wrong one you got.

"You're telling me the doctor says I ought to stay down. He knows I ain't sick as well as I know it. He think I'm gonna hurt myself by this window, gonna jump out of this window? A hundred times a day you come in here to keep the real clothes off me and to keep me on my damn back. Come on, then, and take this rope out of my hands again before you think I'll start tying knots. But I ain't tying no knots, and I ain't climbing out of here. I'm just looking out, looking out at the outside.

"And I could think about apologizing for that juice, you know, if you'd quit holding me back. I'd be almost sorry for spilling it again, even if I have told you every time that I hate that orange juice."

A nurse at each thin shoulder gently turned Leah's narrow face away from the stripes of sun still squeezing through the blinds and led her to bed. One of them pushed Leah under the fresh sheets to rest.

"I ain't gonna be leaving him," she told them. "I ain't gonna be walking out on that boy and leave him here for somebody else to have. He's just got his mama. He's just got him a little house to go back to. If you'd ever let me alone before I rot in this bed, I'd show you. Bring him on in here. Bring him on back so we can stare at him again like we did yesterday, but I'll hold him and take him on out of here so don't laugh about it. Don't be looking around and waiting for me to leave just because he ain't got no arms and no daddy that you know about. I'll get used to my boy by myself."

A nurse, who wasn't listening, marked charts while she watched Leah swallow two blue pills. She told her patient to eat a warm lunch. Leah pulled her knees up under her chin, feeling naked in the hospital gown, figuring that her eyes would roll back in her head in twenty minutes. The pills would, for sure, roll her back in about twenty minutes.

"Bring him on in here for me to feed him lunch. That's what I want. I'll hold him. I'll get used to him before you can think of anything else to do with either one of us. There ain't nothing else for you to do," she told them while they wheeled a plastic lunch tray into her room. She could smell steam from the pale vegetables they wanted to feed her.

"Doctor says you're not quite strong enough yet, honey. Eat a little food. They're taking care of your boy's bottles in the nursery. He's a fine boy, Miss Makes. He's gonna be fine."

When the nurses left, Leah stepped out of bed, holding a blanket around her waist, and piled the damp carrots from her tray onto the middle of her mattress. "They aren't listening to me," she said, walking to the window, slipping her head and shoulders behind the clattering blinds to fall asleep. She wouldn't let them keep her down. She pressed her dry lips against the bright glass, looking out into the town resting under the fresh sun. As the pills slowed her mind, Leah felt the brown drawstring brush her neck and she caught it for support. She tied a loose knot in the rope with heavy fingers. Her eyes crossed with sleep, and they faded back from the clear afternoon light until she saw four or five or six yellow houses with white trim, looking like her own, spinning in the alleys of her town. They spun under the sun, spreading in color behind her flickering eyelids, as she dropped to her knees.

What stuck in her head until the middle of the night was how they said she wasn't strong enough to take care of her boy. She had hardly gotten to see him five minutes after supper, and the way the doctor and the nurses talked to her from the foot of the white bed stayed with her. Their shaking heads stuck with her, swaying in a dream she had early in the night where everything moved from side to side, quietly, with her sleep. The doctor had told her to stay down and still for another day or two, and there he was in her dream, shaking and holding her, with big hands, away from a baby that floated through the black spaces around her body and didn't cry. The big hands, white and damp, were with Leah when she woke up. She knew that baby needed to be staying near her, and she knew she sure as hell was strong enough to make things that way. She didn't need to lie still in her room, dawdling, only thinking about slipping into the halls after the night nurse took her blood pressure. She just went and did it after she put her slippers on. There was no extra consideration.The nursery was in the east wing, and Leah went looking for it in the night. She hugged her arms against her chest for warmth because she couldn't find her robe, and the nurses never had said where they had put it.

The nursery was nearly dark because the attendant was on the main hall heating coffee. Leah walked carefully into the hum of small, warm machines. Respirators and incubators clicked from the edges of the crowded room. Leah's white gown was reflected in glass and hard, clear plastic, and her shadow curled itself over and under the narrow tubes that breathed along the walls. She heard gurgles and the shallow cough of one of the older babies under the hospital drone, but at first, Leah couldn't find them and she kept turning through her own shadows. "Damn, babe," she said, "you ain't that small." A thin wail finally led her to one of the low and open baskets. She watched the black shape of the baby under her eyes try to roll in the dark. It swung its fists at its face with every breath—a new born wriggling in its first night air. Leah turned it on its heaving stomach before she bent down among the other shadow-hidden baskets to find her son. Each small crib was black and quiet, looking the same, so she touched every child she could find, riding her fingers along their smooth necks until she found their shoulders. She reached lightly for each separate skin until she knew her baby from the soft, loose feel above his ribs.

Her son was sleeping quietly on his back in an open crib. His thin pink legs kicked at Leah's arm when she touched him, but he didn't wake up while her long hands ran across his face and belly. Leah rubbed him while he slept; she pressed herself gently into him until she felt like he was really only hers. She pushed the stiff, sterile smells of the hospital away, staring at him through the shadows until she could see each dark hair plastered on his damp forehead. Leah felt herself really love the soft skin that spread under her wide palms. She had been missing it. Smoothing the hard, lost lumps of his empty shoulders freed her angry mind, made her want to cry, made her want to have her son out of the warm, stale air of the nursery. When she took the name bracelet off of his twitching ankle, he groaned in his sleep.

"Come on, babe. Come on," she said to him. "You got to come out of there and see what goes on. You got to learn." She rolled him to one side to get his diaper off after she untied the bows of her gown. "And we got to start up now."

The night nurse found them in the middle of the room when she came back to check on her newborns. Leah stood bare in the night with her short, white gown lying around her feet, nursing her naked son from a brown-tipped breast. She pressed him to her skin where his arms should have been and asked the nurse, in a whisper, not to turn the light on.

"My main question is whether she's fit or not. I hear they think about that at the hospital."

"Well, seeing how the first one died on her, I guess they should think about it. She can't have hardly any money, and I know no daddy's gonna speak up for a child like that one now. I don't wonder at the hospital hesitating. They at least ought to check her house to make sure it's clean."

"Health Department will do it."

"I guess so. You know I'm not positive I trust that girl while I'm looking at her. Maybe can't feed a baby as fast as she can make one."

"Sure she can, Kit. You know it, too. She'll loosen up one

of her short dresses and pull herself right out of the top. Let him suck right there. Might do it on the porch when it's sunny. Might do it in front of us like that, and I wouldn't be surprised. You be ready. Ain't so hard for a girl like that to feed a little one. I don't care if she is thin."

"Gonna be bad to watch it, Mallie."

"Ain't nothing to do but watch it, just watch right out of your window. I'm gonna sit here and look once in a while because I want to see if that yellow-haired boy comes back and tries to park on our side of the street."

"You think he's the one that did it?"

"She's the one that did it. I just want to see if anybody comes back to her little white door."

"Dead babies, babies with no arms ought to stop her, don't you think?"

"No. She ain't made to stop until there's nothing left for her."

"Nothing but a crippled boy?"

"And a few boards to that shack. She'll want to stay there for almost anything. But I think she's bound to lose it. Welfare can't be giving her that much, and her daddy never did save."

"Well, Lord—I reckon that baby might die yet, don't you think?"

"I put no money on him past November."

The paint smell made Leah sick to her stomach, and didn't she already know what it meant to be nauseous a lot of the time? She asked herself that. She told herself she hadn't done anything to earn the extra burden. "Babe, you made me sick enough," she told the bundle napping in the middle of the yard. "I don't want no more of it," she said, and she tried to paint the porch by standing upwind. Her son slept under the afternoon light and her curses while the work went on. "Babe," she called to him when she was doing window sills, "I want you to know that I'm doing this for you and me. I'm doing it with our money, but I can't let you see it close because something could fall on you or something. That's why you're in the yard," she told him. "To keep safe."

It took Leah a week to do the outside. She even trimmed

the rusted old gutters with white paint, spitting down into the grass when the smell and the height of the ladder turned her stomach. She painted every wide board yellow again, asking herself, stroke for stroke, why she didn't change colors. The paint reminded her of Rennie's hair and face—yellow, thick, and dull. "But I can't change much, babe," she told her sleeping son. "You and me are enough of a change, so I got to keep the rest plain. You'll love this house enough like it is. It ain't so bad, and it's mainly all I've got to go with you."

In the evening, she would set the baby on her knees and help him balance his head over his small ribs. She let him rock himself back and forth between her hands while the sky cooled and weighed the hot, stiff smell of the paint down with the dew. She moved with him until he was tired and the street was dark and she could feed him once more in the fresh air, right on the porch. Leah cradled him against her tight breasts until dusk had sunk under the streetlights, humming to herself below the echoing shouts of her neighbor's moving children. She would think of nothing else until she curled around the child on her large, stale mattress with a clean diaper near her hand. She would only wait, looking through her open bedroom window, for her baby to cry, wondering if he was hungry, wet, or aching for the feel of his missing arms. She waited for him to get through every night, drifting into her own sleep with her face toward the opening dawn when she couldn't hold her head up anymore. When she rolled away from her baby, Leah dreamed of her hands painting everything they could reach. She dreamed, then, that she painted everything she knew yellow with the straight ends of her own brown hair.

"Fire Department first."

"Then the Welfare people?"

"But the firemen have got to come on and tell me that her place is a dry wood trap. I'm sure of it. A danger to the neighborhood."

"You really don't like that new paint, do you?"

"The Welfare folks ain't gonna like the fact that her yard ain't got grass for him to play in, and they won't like all that new paint left around for him to drink and chew on."

"He can't hardly move yet, you know."

"She ain't being clean and safe. I don't want my kids getting worms, chasing rats."

"When will they come?"

"Tomorrow. I'm gonna tell them that I think her first one died because of the paint. I'll bet it did."

"You wanting them to take him away?"

"I'd like them to take the whole thing away, but it won't happen. I just really don't trust her because she's been so quiet. Probably ready to drop another baby any week now. They probably march in her back door, ready and waiting at night."

"She's always been quiet. You've never heard nothing."

"Well, I don't sit by this window hour after every hour. But that don't mean it don't happen. I've been watching this morning while she's been cleaning up. Shaking out a new rug, hanging up a line of diapers. Probably getting a visitor tonight."

"You're gonna wear her out in my mind, Mallie. The girl's probably just doing her chores, trying to keep her mind off her crippled baby. Hard job painting all that."

"The Fire Department won't be too much, I know. They expect you to call in about things like this."

"Miss Leah Makes finally gonna know who you are."

"She knows me."

"She's finally gonna get the full eye, I think. And the Welfare people got to be hard to get in touch with. You know that?"

"I know that."

"Ain't had a bit of luck, I'll bet. You want some cream in that coffee?"

"No ma'am. I don't like to thin nothing out."

Rennie drove by once one Saturday while Leah was changing the baby's diapers in the yard. She was on her knees, but she could see his red Chevrolet sliding past the pickets of her freshly white fence. She had heard the car hit the block anyway, carrying the low rumble she would always recognize under its wheels. Rennie drove past her house without stopping, like he used to do just to tease her. He looked straight ahead through his thick, yellow bangs, and it wasn't hard for Leah to tell that he really didn't care. She knew he wouldn't spin back around the block this time, and she sure as hell didn't want him to. Rennie's sister and her red-haired friend, who was trying to squeeze herself onto Rennie's lap, were the ones who stared and started to say something.

"Yooouuuwheee. There's a smell . . .," but Rennie shut them up by jerking the gliding car to the left. The girls were thrown into a corner of the front seat, squealing. Rennie's sister lost her cigarette out of the window. Leah stood straight up and watched them cruise out of sight with her heart beating just a little bit faster. She didn't even try to tell them all to go to hell. She just stared them down until the red rode out of her mind once again. Leah had known that Rennie would be easy to forget. He was too seventeen, too young. He didn't want to know what he'd done. Seeing his flat, blank face shrinking in the rear view mirror only made it easier. In a few more days her heart would finally sink down into a steadiness that matched her breathing. She kissed her baby, who was drying naked in the sunlight at her feet, for being black-haired and thin like his granddaddy. He was just learning to laugh for her, and the warmth of his gurgles pulled her down to lie beside his blankets in the dirt.

"Babe," she told him, "your damn daddy just slipped through your life." She pulled her dress up on her thighs to feel the sun while she watched the baby roll himself over and over by kicking his legs. He was getting along on his own. "Be glad," she told him.

"We was only mainly concerned that there ain't no grass in your yard."

"I planted plenty of seed when we got back from the hospital."

"We was only afraid your baby might get hurt."

"No baby of mine gonna get hurt in my own yard."

"Honey, it has happened before."

"That ain't none of your business. She stopped breathing one morning while she was lying in the shade. Doctor says it happens a lot."

"Ain't never happened to me. What was you feeding her?"

"Mallie, that's got nothing to do with . . . ."

"It's all my own business. Me and my baby are just fine. We got grass growing in our yard. The house ain't burning and ain't likely to start since I'm here every day."

"You know, Miss Makes, how they're always checking these things. No reason to get mad."

"I expect they're coming to your place tomorrow. Coming to look for rats?"

"No reason to be mad."

"Yes ma'am, we just wanted everything to be all right."

"We only wanted to see how you and your boy have been getting along."

"Doing fine on our own, and we ain't done nothing to have firemen and the Welfare on our backs."

"We're glad to know it's all fine."

"Don't need too many neighbors on my back."

"Well, we're sorry for . . . ."

"What do you call that boy, honey? He's a nice boy from what I can see from here."

"To you he's Mister Makes, calling him after his granddaddy."

"Nice."

"Nice to name a boy after his granddaddy."

Leah spent the whole night looking for them out of her front window. Across the street, the kitchen light went out early. Leah saw Mallie's friend, Kit, walk through the hedges to her own home before the air was completely black. But she stayed awake, staring at the blue street lights reflecting in Mallie's windows until the baby woke up for his four o'clock feeding. She knew for sure now how she couldn't trust any of them. They sure as hell had been watching her every minute. They'd been looking out of their holes to make something of her.

Probably just dying to know who his daddy is, she told herself. Probably just dying to know how he can float in his bath with no arms.

She came up with the idea of leaving him in Mallie's yard when she saw that she would have to fix the roof by herself. It would show them how he wasn't so delicate, wasn't so likely to die at any second. It would show how he could move right into other people's lives. "Now don't you be afraid or nothing, babe. I'm just moving you across the street so I can see you when I'm on the roof. You'll be right where I can always see you. And I'm keeping plenty of rocks in my pocket for your protection. The ladies are worrying about you, but ain't none of them gonna do anything to you before I start throwing stones," she told him. "The grass is better over there anyway, they say."

"You just let them look at you hard and long. Don't think about it. It should only take me a couple of hours to nail those new shingles in place."

"She was wearing that same print dress when I saw her on the roof and that damned little boy was wiggling in my yard."

"Well now, fixing her roof in that nice dress."

"And leaving that baby and his blankets by my fence where she could see him."

"What did you think of it?"

"What do you mean what did I think? The boy ain't got no arms and he was lying in my yard. And she stared down at me the whole time I was outside looking at him."

"Did she talk?"

"Not a word to me. Just bending over her roof in that dress. She was hammering up there, but I know, too, that she was keeping one big eye on me."

"How long did she leave him?"

"Most of the morning. Most of two, three hours."

"Didn't cry or scream or anything?"

"Not a peep from him. I felt like I had to make sure he was alive after a while. I wouldn't have put it past her to leave him dead out there the way she is. She don't like me."

'What did you do to the boy? Pinch him? Feed him something?"

"Nothing much. I just poked him under the chin with a little stick until he woke up. He still didn't cry."

"And she threw a rock at you?"

"Landed right on the porch. And then, she had the nerve to keep on hammering up there with one hand in her pocket. Never looked back at me."

"Lucky she didn't hit you."

"Lucky I didn't take that baby downtown to the Welfare myself. He looks sick to me, too."

"You wouldn't have gotten nothing done down there, Mallie. I told you that."

"Well, that don't matter. I still ain't got no respect left for a girl that treats a baby like that. He don't even have a real name. That's what really gets to me."

Rennie didn't see the baby at first. He was spitting between his boots, listening to his sister whine over the dirty dishes while the white bundle breathed at the foot of the porch steps. Rennie noticed it when he spit on it and the glow of the blankets in the damp dirt spread to his face. When he picked it up in his greasy hands, he knew it was a baby.

"Mama. Mama and Em, come out here quick. Somebody's left us a baby in the yard."

He nearly dropped the child handing it to his sister. "Mama," he said, "I don't know what about it, but here it is. It's a goddam baby and I found it right in the yard."

"Well, it's alive and looking hungry," Em said, and she showed her mama the thin, kicking legs she was unwrapping.

"Is it all right?" Rennie asked. "Has somebody left us something like that?" He watched the women strip the child under the glare of the porch light. When the naked baby finally screamed out from Em's arms, nobody said a word. Rennie's mama turned her back. Em held the child under its ribs and let it hang like a stunned rabbit from between her hands.

"You take a look at this, Rennie, and tell me what you think. I just see a black-headed baby with no arms right here."

"Do something with him, Rennie," his mama said before she went back into the house.

"Do something? What am I supposed to do? He ain't my fault."

"Just don't leave him where the dogs can reach," Em said. "His mama's sure to come after him sometime. Everybody says she loves him to death."

Rennie carried his son out into the driveway, holding the restless, moving body between his outstretched hands. He couldn't stand to hold it or think about it. He prayed over his straining, greasy palms that it wouldn't cry all night and that it wouldn't die on their property where he would have to bury it. He left the bundle, balanced and warmly-wrapped, on the hood of his red Chevrolet, feeling all the time like there were eyes looking for him from the woods. "You don't belong to me," he said loudly in the dark. "You ain't my fault."

Leah carried her son down off the ridge and back to town slung on her shoulders in a web of old diapers. "Babe, I am sorry to keep you up so late," she said to him as he was swayed into a fitful sleep by her steps. "I am almost even sorry I let him touch you. But I felt like it had to be. Some things just go like that. That boy needs to see what goes on without him. His mama needs to see it. His bitch sister needs to see it."

"They had to know what you are by yourself, without you hardly making a sound." Leah reached over her shoulders to steady the baby as she turned at the bottom of the hill toward the quiet edge of town. "I am proud."

"There ain't but one more person that ought to catch a strong sight of you."

Leah kept to the unlit streets on the way to the graveyard. She wanted to hold the two of them silent and hidden together in the summer night. "I know this is asking a lot of you, babe, knowing how it's late and empty in this dark. But this means a little bit to me," she said, stepping and wading through the broken, sunken ground patched with sharp-edged headstones. "This does mean something special for me."

Leah lay the baby in a small hollow of ground wedged near the roots of an old tree. She could just see his pale face wrinkle sleepily in the curve of the blankets when she moved him. "I reckon I might leave you right here for a minute, babe, and see what you think. She was so little when she stopped breathing that she fit right in this spot. It does surprise me how much it's sunk already, and I do wish to God that I had the money for a real marker. This thing," she said, pointing to a wooden stake at the edge of the small grave, "is only to keep them from using her spot over again."

"Do you reckon," she asked, with her heart beating through the air between them, "that you might lie here for a while and finish getting a feel for the family? My daddy always wished he could lie here, but he didn't have a cent. I wish sometimes," she said, "that I still did have a whole family. In one armful, you know, like you might imagine."

Leah wandered before she finally sat on a low concrete tomb, a few dark yards away from her daughter's grave, to watch her baby. Her mind kept streaming to her, talking through the loneliness of the quiet, the past deaths. Her son lay, almost still, in the night shade of the tree for an hour. She moved toward him, through the wet grass and stone, only after she felt like he must have had his time.

"Babe, I first got to let you know that I really don't like having her here, and I bet she don't like being here either. I want you to know that," she said, kissing her baby's damp forehead while a light wind blew changing shadows past them. Her words broke over him. "The second thing I already know, though, is how you would have really liked her. She was a good one."

"You probably would have liked her daddy, too, babe, when I think about it. He was a fine man. I always wish I had seen him again after that third or fourth time."

Leah kept a rag tied around her own forehead the whole time she tended to his fever. "Yeah, babe. Here we are, babe," she said to him. "Just you and me playing Indian. Here we are, playing in the desert, singing and sharing water."

She bent over him, she sang to him, she held him close while he burned and cried until he was hoarse. At night, she slid cool, damp cloths across her son's brow and body, again and again. She couldn't see the angry splashing of his rash in the moonlight, and she made herself forget, in her fatigue, the distant, ugly twitches of his limbs. He was beautiful—taller than he had been—and his eyes, in their fever, were so deep. Leah recognized, hour after hour, how his legs and feet were shaped like her own. He had her knees, he had her long calves. And before the mornings broke, she found herself cupping and molding his flesh, hoping for a change. One toe, two toes, three toes—she caressed his tiny joints while he tossed, and always, always, she felt him to be as strong and cool as ivory.

"Maybe it would be easier if I knew where you babies sucked up all these germs," she said while she bathed him. "But I don't. I guess they're all around. Bad luck for us, I guess. They're all around."

When he died in the heat of the summer, when his lungs finally couldn't pull fresh air past his first measles fever, Leah wanted to bury her son like she had wanted to bury her daughter. But she couldn't do it. She went to the corner of the house, next to the foundation. She took a shovel out there and tried to dig a hole in the rain one hundred and fifty-seven days after he was born. The digging was easy, but the neighbor's dog howled through the wet night while Leah lifted the light mud over her shoulder, and her mind kept saying that the dogs would get him, they would get him.

So she wrapped him and waited to start giving him up like she'd waited since he squeezed himself loose from between her legs. "Babe," she told him, "you are mostly right to pass on, I guess. It wouldn't be so good for a boy with no arms. You wouldn't have liked it much."

Leah rocked him between her trembling hands until the dry morning cut through the windows and washed the last shadow of color from her son's sinking face. "I was going to bury you nearly under the house, babe," she told him while she moved out to the porch. "But I know how something might dig you up, might pull you out to look at and play with. I couldn't take that." She pulled one blanket away from his legs because the air was warm. He felt lighter and lighter in her arms. "I can only think of laying you out next to your sister. There might be room. I reckon that it wouldn't be the worst."

She didn't cry, but the porch finally did close in on her. "Too hot under here, babe. I'm for moving into the breeze." A few minutes before lunch, Leah sat down on the edge of the street with the baby rolling loose in her arms. She sweat through the early afternoon heat. "There's really nowhere I can take you, babe. There really ain't much for me to do at this minute. I've got no luck and no motion but to see it come and go right past me.

"We should probably sit still right here. It'll sure be all out of our hands soon."

"Ain't you glad you finally did call that ambulance?"

"It's a blessing. The whole damn thing is."

"A final blessing that he did die. Hmmm, Lord. I been waiting for it."

Madonna on Her Back

Every evening Joelle had to bribe Ellis all to hell to get her to sit still.

"I'll wash the dishes. I'll do nearly every one of Annie's diapers this weekend," she'd say. "Just don't shift everything so much. When you move, the shadows change."

"Well," her sister would say to her, "I can tell you ain't had a baby chew on you five or six times a day. If you had, you would know what it's like."

"It's true," Joelle would answer. "It hasn't happened to me. Might never happen. I just want us to both do the best we can. Please."

"Okay." Ellis would try to be patient. "But can I switch her now?"

"Sure. You might have to undo the last button for this side though. Your blouse is in the way." And Ellis would gently turn her daughter from one breast to the other while Joelle stared and sketched in the failing light.

Joelle loved her sister for her tolerance. Ellis would give her forty-five minutes, an hour, of drawing time before Annie went to bed and the television was turned on. And she gave it away without understanding it. She'd say things like "I sure as hell wish I knew why you're so hot about my mothering, heat rash and all," or "Lord, you can tell I haven't got a man anymore. Nothing but babies and naked women in this house." And she would play the big sister for Joelle, talking right at her while Annie nursed. "J. babes," she'd say, "we've got to find you somebody. We need to get you a hairy chest, some late night dancing, somebody to treat you and teach you nice before you peak." But if Joelle didn't say anything, didn't keep the talk up, Ellis would look down at herself or Annie's earnest puckered face, and she'd fade out. Joelle, working quietly with her pencils, would try to catch it—memories, the pangs of a labor pushed through alone, a passing fear of old age—as her sister sadly bit her lip, the question "Do I sag? Am I sagging?" crinkling across her brow and quivering beneath her collarbones.

Joelle had tried, once or twice, to let Ellis know what the extra drawing time meant to her. It wasn't just that she needed a break after hours of supervising construction paper and finger paint. It wasn't even so much that her sister was beautiful. Ellis's face lacked the distinction, her features lacked the strength that Joelle most admired. Still, she wanted to draw what she knew. She had tried before to say, "Hey, Ellis, you know I'm not after your baby or wasting your time. I don't have the equipment for that. I just like to draw you, you know, because you're alive and . . . well, it's hard to say . . . but after Bern and all, looking at you is looking at a real woman." She had also tried to say that she would like to be a little bit the same. But, instead, as their dinners settled and baby sucked mama dry, it usually came down to Joelle's remark that Ellis was a cheap and easy model, Ellis's wondering about whose "goddam snug Levi's" Bern was in, and Annie's bedtime.

One night, while the smell of their homemade chicken broth still hung over the kitchen counter, Ellis tried to change their lives. Joelle was working on her sister's profile, feeling out the curve of the cheek and the tight setting of the eye. It was a sketch of tension without Annie, without motherhood. Joelle was so caught up in her lines and thoughts of color . . . Lord, Ellis, if only you were dark brown or olive-skinned, how lovely it would be . . . that she wasn't ready for ideas.

"I think I've got to do it, Joelle. I mean I think we've got to do it. This big house and not too much money. You don't really make that much, you know. Well, we wouldn't even have to paint the end room. Not really. We could just air it out, put a nicer chair by the window, and rent it in a snap."

Joelle heard her but let the talking slide by. She'd gotten it into her head that she couldn't capture Ellis's eye in pencil and that only paint—deep, muddy paint—would do the trick. Her hands warmed with eagerness as her sister talked. It had been a while. She had never been great with oils. But they were the answer—she could see and smell that. Ellis would really come alive on canvas.

"I guess I really do think the end room is best, J. I figure the farther away from Annie the better. She still cries at night sometimes. Of course, you're the one who's going to have to share a bathroom. I mean, unless we start sending people downstairs. What do you think? You think another person would be in the way?"

"No," Joelle answered carefully, playing with drawn ideas of her sister's hair as short and curly. "I guess it doesn't really bother me. It would be hard to bother me. I don't do much outside the classroom and this kitchen."

"Well, they'll have to be clean and they'll have to be quiet. And I sure don't plan on fixing all their meals."

Joelle asked her if they needed the money.

"Hundred, hundred and fifty a month for a clean place in town. All utilities. Washer and dryer. Couldn't hurt us a bit though it would give me something else to worry about, something to go with this noisy bundle Annie."

But are you lonely?, Joelle wanted to ask. Are you tired and afraid of thinking back on Bern every afternoon? The idea of a boarder didn't strike Joelle with anything like the force of her sister's sadness. She watched Ellis play with the undone buttons of her blouse while the baby slept across her knees. She wondered what it was like to be twenty-eight or nine and left behind. If Ellis wanted a boarder to fuss after, she probably ought to have one.

"Okay," Joelle said, closing her drawing pad and wiping her smudged hands on her pants, "if you can find somebody you want and somebody who wants us, I'm willing to give it a try. But you'll have to cut a deal with me. I want to paint you. I want to draw you up permanently in oils with your baby. You'll have to sit still for that."

"Oh sure," Ellis said, laughing. "Sure, I'll sit still for you for two or three years. Come on. Are you serious?"

"Yes."

"How long?"

"An hour, an hour and a half a night for our boarder's first month."

"Oh great. I sit down here every night after the news with my tits hanging out in the cold. Our boarder will love that. He'll really love it."

"He?"

"Oh sure. I really think it ought to be a man. Don't you? Better wage earner and all that."

Of course, Ellis took the first fellow that came by. But Joelle didn't let it get to her. She reasoned that no man Ellis might accept would be worse than the next, and besides, the boarder was Ellis's game to play. She had cleaned the back bedroom; she had gotten a full month's rent in advance. And she seemed, to Joelle, to be happy in her preoccupation. When Joelle came home from school with sheaves of student drawings in her arms to find boxes in the hall and new curtains in the bathroom, she took it all in stride. She let the new scent, the sweet smell of their boarder's packed belongings, spread into her life with no comment. She was going to paint Ellis; she was going to practice on her sister and fill the kitchen with her own oily smell. She would meet the new boarder, but she wouldn't care about him.

Ellis still went right to work on her. "Well, it's true he's young and in college and not making his own money. And I know it's risky to take the first one. Let me get all that up front first," she said. "But I couldn't help liking him, and his bill-paying parents sound stable. He looks clean and responsible and okay to me, Joelle. I'm really happy with the whole thing."

Joelle agreed that everything sounded fine. She noticed her sister was kneading her special whole wheat bread dough, probably for dinner.

"His name is Will, William Kramer. I've invited him down for supper. Just this once, you know," she said while she shaped her loaves. "He needs a little time to settle in. He's just barely twenty-one and this is his first time out of the college dormitories. And J., wait till you catch on to his blue eyes. Mmmm."

Joelle laughed with her sister, keeping her ideas to herself. "How does he feel about living with us women and our baby and our early hours?" she asked, watching her sister's hands mold and caress, knowing now who the bread was being made for.

"Oh, he didn't mind the idea, but he did say it would be new for him. He's never had a sister or anything. And you know what I told him, J.? He's young, and I want to get along, you know. I told him he could have girls upstairs to visit. I sure don't care." Ellis chuckled to herself. She laughed and covered the loaves so they could rise in their pans. "I guess I pretty much told this college fella to go at it as long as he was quiet."

Joelle turned toward the family room. She remembered how the scents, the brands of soap, the shuffles and murmurs would double. The house would warm up and move again. Her hands lay cold in her lap. It had been a long time since she had thought of Fleming without warning. She thought she had washed him out for a good while.

"You don't mind do you, J.?" Ellis ran some water in the sink. "It seems only fair to me."

Dinner was warm and wholesome. Annie was sleepy. Joelle and Ellis were more than polite. And Will, the boarder, was really thankful for the homemade soup and bread. Ellis tried hard to work them all into comfortable conversation. She chattered on about parents and bread-making, and she even talked about the college some though it wasn't a place she really cared about. Joelle smiled, looked at her new housemate from the corner of her eye, and began drawing him, steadily, in the back of her mind while he ate and wiped his hands on the linen napkin spread across his lap.

Tinting the male eyes blue, shaping the long fingers, Joelle had to admit that she was curious to know a little more. Young Mr. Kramer, she noticed, mentioned only what he saw, and since he saw no wedding rings, no photos, no extra place setting at the table, his comments about the house, Annie, and the pair of sisters who served the meal as a wandering tandem were light and innocuous. He was handsome—no, Joelle decided it was pretty—he was a pretty, gentle, shy-looking fellow. He was a boy to her, really, when she thought about it except that he did seem a little bit poised while he sat at their small kitchen table; he did seem to know a thing or two. But Ellis, Joelle thought, Ellis is reading him like he's a man. She's just waiting for him to slip a free hand under the table. Joelle watched her sister breathe closely over the shoulder of their boarder as she asked him if he'd like seconds. She could feel Ellis measuring his waist, tracing the length of his legs.

While they were finishing Ellis's freshly brewed coffee, Will noticed the pads and erasers that Joelle kept stacked in the kitchen corner.

"Oh, yes," Ellis said, "Joelle teaches art, day in and day out, at the local elementary school. Finger paint, magic marker, clay—you wouldn't believe the stuff that's on her hands and clothes when she comes in the door from there." Ellis sat herself down beside the guest.

"I see. You all are the kind of ladies that bring your work home with you." The boarder warmed up to them, lightly, innocuously.

"Joelle sure does," Ellis said. "My job right now is here with Annie. She's a beauty, isn't she? That stuff over there, though, is for our new painting. My sister keeps her school work upstairs."

Young Mr. Kramer thought he had hit upon a hobby to get comfortable with. Joelle watched his pleased hands slip into his pockets. "So you two paint together. Do you use the same subject, the same still life or something like that?"

"Oh, no," Ellis continued. "My sister's the only painter." Joelle felt herself blush while Ellis talked on. The painting was such a new idea; she wasn't ready to have it slapped onto the table, and there Ellis was nailing everything down in public. "Joelle is going to paint me and Annie."

"It's really just something extra to do," Joelle interjected.

"She's got it figured out though. A real mother and daughter scene. My sitting still for it is part of a deal." Ellis laughed. "She gets the painting, and I get a boarder. So, now I've got you to go with this whole mess," and she waved her hand over the after-dinner clutter of the counters and Joelle's painting corner. "Quite a trade, I think."

Will Kramer got himself out of Joelle's embarrassment by

stacking his coffee saucer on his dessert plate, rattling things and trying to be helpful. "Well, I'll stay out of your way. Just tell me when you don't want me in the kitchen."

"That's all right," Joelle said. "Don't worry about it. It's nothing really." She took his silverware from him.

"I wouldn't quite say that, Joelle. It means a lot to you. I think Will ought to know how we'll be in here after dinner in case he wants some coffee or something." Ellis laughed again. "I reckon we could hang a big sign on the door."

The sisters made their new boarder excuse himself from the dishes. They both felt they needed to talk alone. Joelle let Ellis know that her painting shouldn't be made into such a big deal. "This is the first one in a while for me, Ellis. I just can't quite be sharing my hopes with people other than you. Let's keep this a quiet thing."

But hostess Ellis had wound herself past excitement and into a huff. She was frustrated that she hadn't worked Will Kramer quite right, that he had been embarrassed and that Joelle had, maybe, made it worse. "Well, at least I didn't tell him the real thing. At least I didn't tell him I'd be undressed in here while my sister stared at me. Men don't like that kind of thing, you know, Joelle. They don't take to it at all. What's he gonna think? What's our college man gonna think about two locked-up bitches who do nothing but cook and strip down and watch over some baby? He'll think we're sick."

"Only Bern would think we were sick."

"Forget him," Ellis yelled.

"Glad to," said Joelle, and she turned her back to start washing soup bowls in the sink.

"I'm just not willing to be different, Joelle. Not even for you. I don't have it in me." Ellis moved toward her baby, who was whining in the crib. They both felt it—the lock and bolt of living together. Joelle's hands shook a little as she buried them in dishwater. She knew it; she'd known it. Ellis would only really undress herself for, she'd only really show herself to a fast-breathing man. Ellis herself ran her fingers through her hair like she was remembering what Bern's eyes had looked like under her touch. "I don't have much in me lately," she said.

Joelle began with a series of light pencil sketches on a night when their boarder was attending a late class. She wanted to work toward a composition and a pose that was easy, comfortably natural, for all of them. Ellis had, in her last twitch of stubbornness, worn a light blue pullover which she shoved up under her armpits so Annie could get to her. It would have been easier, Joelle thought, if she'd stuck to a cotton blouse, but Ellis's painting, like so many things, was becoming Ellis's show. Big sister wan't so convinced that her modelling was sick since Will Kramer wasn't out and Joelle had been so patient with her promise. Still, it was her face, her body, her baby.

For a while, until her back got tired, she faced Joelle squarely with the thin sweater bunched under her chin and her stomach sucked back from the tight waistline of her jeans. But as Annie nursed quietly on and Joelle sketched without a word, she gave it up. She would simply be defiant, still young, and turbulent around the edges. Joelle was pleased to see that even Ellis couldn't dig up a reason to quarrel out loud when the house and the time were their's alone.

Joelle found her rhythm just as a satiated and burped Annie began to fall asleep in her mother's lap. She drew Ellis's free hand tracing the roundness of her daughter's cheek and kneading the tight curl of her toes. She studied Ellis leaning over Annie, much of her face disappearing in the shadow of her long, thick hair as she crooned, whispered, sang promises through her breaths. Joelle even outlined their movement because as they swayed together—mother and child—the strength of her possibility, her painting, became knotted in their wrapped shapes. She saw it: her own hands shaping Ellis's breasts—rose-tipped, firm, and patched with flush from her daughter's grasp—as they swung lightly under the sharp color of the sweater and the steady rock of shoulders. She would blend those colors with her thumbs while her own lank bangs fell across her eyes and the cool night air tightened the small mounds on her chest. She would highlight, perfectly, the soft face of a mother who never thought to cover herself as her babble became song . . . Jesus loves us, yes, I know . . . and her baby closed its eyes with fingers caught up in its own. Joelle felt herself fall in love one more time. Her fingers ached with inspiration and speed.

Fleming—his wide, clumsy mouth, his blank, ass-pinching eyes—was nothing. Bern was a bastard. Her own wishes mixed with the mottled stains on her palms and wrists. There was real passion in the quiet of a girl's loss, a mama's gain, she thought. Not a breast or a leg or a last sweet smile would really ever change.

Joelle didn't mean to meet up with Will Kramer on the porch the next evening. She had only gone out there, in the dark, to feel the space of the night and match it to her own. She was thinking of her parents—the memories usually so completely flattened in the pictures on the mantelpiece—and watching the moon rise with the breeze as Will Kramer came up the sidewalk. She could tell immediately that he was glad he'd found her alone in the shadows. It was in the way he stopped just short of the house, readjusting his backpack as if he needed to be able to breathe more easily. Mr. Kramer, Joelle thought as she smelled beer and cigarettes in his hurried greeting, there is still something dangerously young about you.

"Nice night," he said, walking past where she sat on the steps so he could leave his books by the door.

"Yes," she said, still facing the yard. "Ellis and I have always loved sitting on this porch, taking things in."

"Ellis," he said, moving to sit one step above her, his jacket rustling like he was looking for his cigarettes. "Is your sister planning on coming out later?"

Joelle smiled. "No, I don't think so," she answered. "She's with the baby."

"Do you mind if I stay out here then? Keep you company?" Joelle was surprised because he touched her, with his knee, right when he asked her, right when a match flared white in his palm. It might have been an accident. And she knew that it didn't mean much anyway. Every man she'd met would push himself loose if his chance was framed in darkness and the sweet silence of a woman he didn't know, didn't have to look at. But she hadn't expected it. It occurred to her, at that very second, that he was going for her. The boy was going for her.

"I guess not," she answered, her chin in her palms. "But I won't be out much longer."

"That's okay," he said, sliding down a step to be right next to her. "I promise not to be very demanding."

They talked for a while—about school, art, the job market. He confessed he'd been drinking, that drinking made him say things and do things that he had a hard time getting through otherwise. "Oh, I'm not drunk," he said. "But I can look at you. I can tell you, straight out, that I find you interesting."

"Thanks," she said, laughing a little. "I could say the same of you."

He tilted his head back, away from her, as he flicked his cigarette out into the night. "I could also mention that I'm pretty lonely," he said.

The talk died right then, when he pressed his thigh against her calf and felt for her hand. Her heart beat a little faster when he brushed against her, but nothing really moved, nothing melted away. Will Kramer, his profile frozen as he reached for her fingers, couldn't really touch her that way.

"You know," she finally said. "I should be going on inside."

He still tried to kiss her, just after she stood up to stretch, free herself of the kinks. She smiled as she noticed the light from Ellis's second-story bedroom window cutting a bright square onto the lawn. She saw it over Will's shoulder as he hugged her too quickly, without checking her eyes. And she watched the blurred shadows of Ellis putting Annie to bed as Mr. Kramer finally began to sense the stiffness in her back for what it was.

She let him find her lips once before he picked up his backpack and went inside. He kissed her openly, directly—like he was ready for anything. But she didn't move. Ellis is going to laugh and laugh, Joelle thought.

She imagined her sister saying, "J. honey, I can't believe you let that fresh hungry one go." She imagined Ellis twitching her hips and moaning like the loss of a man's touch was death. She only hoped that Will wouldn't feel cheated. A house with two women and bad memories isn't likely to be the loving place for him, she thought.

The next morning Ellis got on a quick high horse Joelle hadn't expected.

"I only have two things to say to you, Joelle, as I can't be saying too much to a girl who ought to be old enough to see trouble where it lies. Two things. First, it's not my business, just like that other fellow wasn't my business. The two of us—we live together, but we are each our own self. You can do what you want—noise and that stuff isn't going to bother me—but I want you to think about what it means to snarl up our business proposition."

"Wait a minute, Ellis." Joelle dropped her spoon against the edge of her cereal bowl. "Hold it. One more practical thing before you jump on me like I know you're going to. I clean his room, so I know one more thing. I know there's a picture, a pretty big one, of a girl on his dresser. She may be a fake blond, she may be a real old girlfriend, but it's still there. You need to think about that."

"Goddamn it, Ellis. You are exasperating. What have you been doing? Hanging out the window listening to every word? As if I cared anyway. You know me better." Joelle gritted her teeth. She told herself she should have been ready, should have understood how her sister's loss and boredom were likely to turn her.

Ellis poured two cups of coffee. "I know enough to think that you might not be remembering Fleming and what he did to you after a while. I let him crash through your door here like he must have crashed through the one you had at college. But I don't really care who you let crawl on top of you. I've made my mistakes and had my quick times too, you know. Let's just say that I don't know whether you should be messing with a paying boarder. That's the real point. We can't very well charge somebody rent if he's not using his room."

"Ellis, he hasn't even been in my room. Relax."

"Okay. I know I shouldn't be all over my twenty-three year old sister. But let me just say that I know what it's like to have a man and lose a man. And I know how a lot of it can come rushing back to you, running up and down your legs in the middle of the night, if you think about it. Just be careful, J." Ellis gave her sister a long look that seemed to rise from the spot where she kept that last day—tears falling on the stairs and one last bruise from Bern visible on her arm—held tight between her spine and her empty womb. She wanted past that.

Joelle could see how she wanted past that. "Just be careful," she said as her eyes reached further and further. "Neither one of us is ready to leap free yet. I don't think you or I could do it because I know, I'm really afraid that I know, there's nobody out there to catch us."

But Ellis couldn't hold herself back. Joelle felt her try once or twice. She felt her try to squeeze herself into a gentle pose with her daughter. But she was restless—her eyes spread tension, her feet smacked uneven rhythms on the floor. Finally, Joelle decided to cut her as loose as she could, to step right off to the side. No more painting for a while. No more over-the-shoulder looks. She would just let her sister go.

She asked Ellis for one more night and got her brushes ready. She figured that a few more strokes in the right places would give her what she needed to finish. Sure, it would be a picture of Ellis, but it would be Ellis—quiet, smiling, hugging a baby—going in one direction. Joelle imagined roughening the hands with a bit more age, lightening the eyes with the smallest pits of anger before calling it quits. I've gotten what I can, she thought.

Ellis herself remained even truer to the speed of her changes. When Joelle walked into the kitchen to set up her easel, she found her sister stretched out, stark naked, on the kitchen table. She had to stop moving for a minute.

"Hello, J. I guess I thought I ought to end this whole thing with a bang. Especially after the fuss I made about taking my shirt off." She laughed. "So, what do you think?"

Joelle, ready to the minute to give her sister over to foolishness and a chase for pride, said nothing. It was a beautiful sight, beautiful and crazy. Ellis's body was marked with all the things Joelle loved—easy curves, stretch marks, the fading boundaries of a borrowed bathing suit, a knee scarred on a childhood across a softening thigh. But she was out of place—in the wrong kitchen at the wrong time. She's only acting this way, Joelle told herself, for the look of some man.

"I guess I do look a little fat, huh? Having a baby will do it to you," Ellis said, glancing critically at her legs, breaking the silence. "Bern, you know, almost always undressed me in the dark."

"Why?" Joelle asked. "Why are you like this tonight? Why don't you just wait?" She turned away. Her hand was sweating around the middle of her brushes, and her fingers felt a little numb. She knew, she was afraid she knew, that Ellis was trying really hard to give something to her.

"I'm doing it because I'm losing it, Joelle, and I want to take a good look backward before I go too far." Ellis sat up and hung her legs over the edge of the table, but she made no effort to cover herself. She drew one finger along the puckered scar of her knee as she talked. "You and I both know what I'm going to do. I'm going out there later to lay Will Kramer down beside the legs of our mama's piano like he's never been laid before. I've wanted to do it since he moved in, and no matter what you think, I think he's been asking for it. Stares at my chest now like it was in a magazine."

Joelle laughed in irritation. "I guess everybody does that to you, Ellis," she said.

"Well, maybe. But as you can see, there's more to me than two good handfuls. A whole lot more. And before I leave here, I want you to know that I'm not going anywhere too far."

Joelle was moved. Every shade of Ellis's pale nakedness moved her. There she was undressed and playing the big sister, while some real part of her was caught up by the thought of a blue-eyed boy. It looked like a waste to Joelle—a big sincere waste. Here Ellis was using more energy to cut another deal. Here she was using her best self to sell Joelle on a bad idea. "I was all ready to let you go, Ellis. Go on. But I know that Will Kramer isn't worth even one of your handfuls, and it bothers me." She moved to set up her easel, not able to look at her sister's swinging legs or the way the age was beginning to settle in her hips. "You're so damned blind you never even look past their belt buckles."

Joelle watched Ellis take it in. Her sister stood up, eyes large in the dim kitchen light, and looked for her shirt. Maybe it was hard for her, Joelle thought. Maybe it was harder than she figured for Ellis to move between the feelings she had for her family and the ache she wanted to push away beneath a heavy pair of legs.

"Oh hell, J. You act like you're jealous. Of course there's no balance. There never is. I'll always count on you, dote on Annie, and keep trying to find someone who will love the breath right out of me. Bern always said that I stuck to him like glue." Ellis sighed. "I'm just too weak to be fair. I'm way too weak."

Joelle wanted to take her judgment back. It wasn't worth it. "I'm sorry," she said. "I shouldn't talk that way. I, of all people, ought to know better."

"The hell you should. Fleming was a creep, but he wasn't as creepy as Bern. He never did really get inside of you and rip you up. Thank God. Don't be asking for a baby and a load of mistakes to make you smarter. It doesn't work. I'm looking for some cheap peace, but there's no way I'll ever want you to get this low."

"You're not low, Ellis." Joelle had managed to set her painting on the easel even though she didn't expect to work on it. Not now. She busied herself, frowning, by picking the scattered clothes off the floor. "Your life's not over."

"No. But I'm past looking for perfect thrills." Ellis stood before her sister with a stubborness held firm by the arms tightly folded across her chest. Her eyes seemed to Joelle to be falling back toward the memory of bruises. But the sight of a nipple—tender and soft—peeking out from the crease of a sharply set elbow was enough to make Joelle laugh and cry her way through things. Ellis, Ellis, she thought, you are still what you don't think you can be. Mama. Sister. You just can't get rid of it.

Joelle helped her sister dress. Ellis said everything had to be just right. "When he comes in," she said, "I'm going to be buttoned up and ready." So Joelle hooked her into a heavy nursing bra, straightened the collar of her blouse, and held her jeans while Ellis looked for her sandals. She told Ellis that she would stay upstairs for the evening and that the painting was going with her. "I'm nearly finished now. I can do without a last sitting for a while. We should wait. Let things settle down a little."

"I'm not breaking my promise, you know, J. Not yet anyway. That painting will get finished." Ellis was brushing her long hair away from her face with Annie's tiny pink hairbrush. "And then we'll start another one, and I'm not kidding. When we've got time, I want you to do a picture of me however you want. I meant all that a while ago. I don't take my clothes off in daylight for just anybody."

But Joelle made her stop. "Please don't try to make any more deals," she said. "I don't like what you're doing, but I'll live with it."

"Well," said Ellis, as she lifted her daughter from the crib, "if you want to stare at and love every inch of me anytime soon, I'll probably be ready not long after I remember how itchy that living room rug is."

The feeling between them was bundled and shifted in the weight of the sleeping child that Ellis handed to Joelle for the evening.

"Remember," Ellis said, "to check her diapers before you go to sleep."

"You just remember to keep it quiet," Joelle reminded Ellis as she carried Annie toward her bedroom. "I'm trying to hold a family together upstairs."

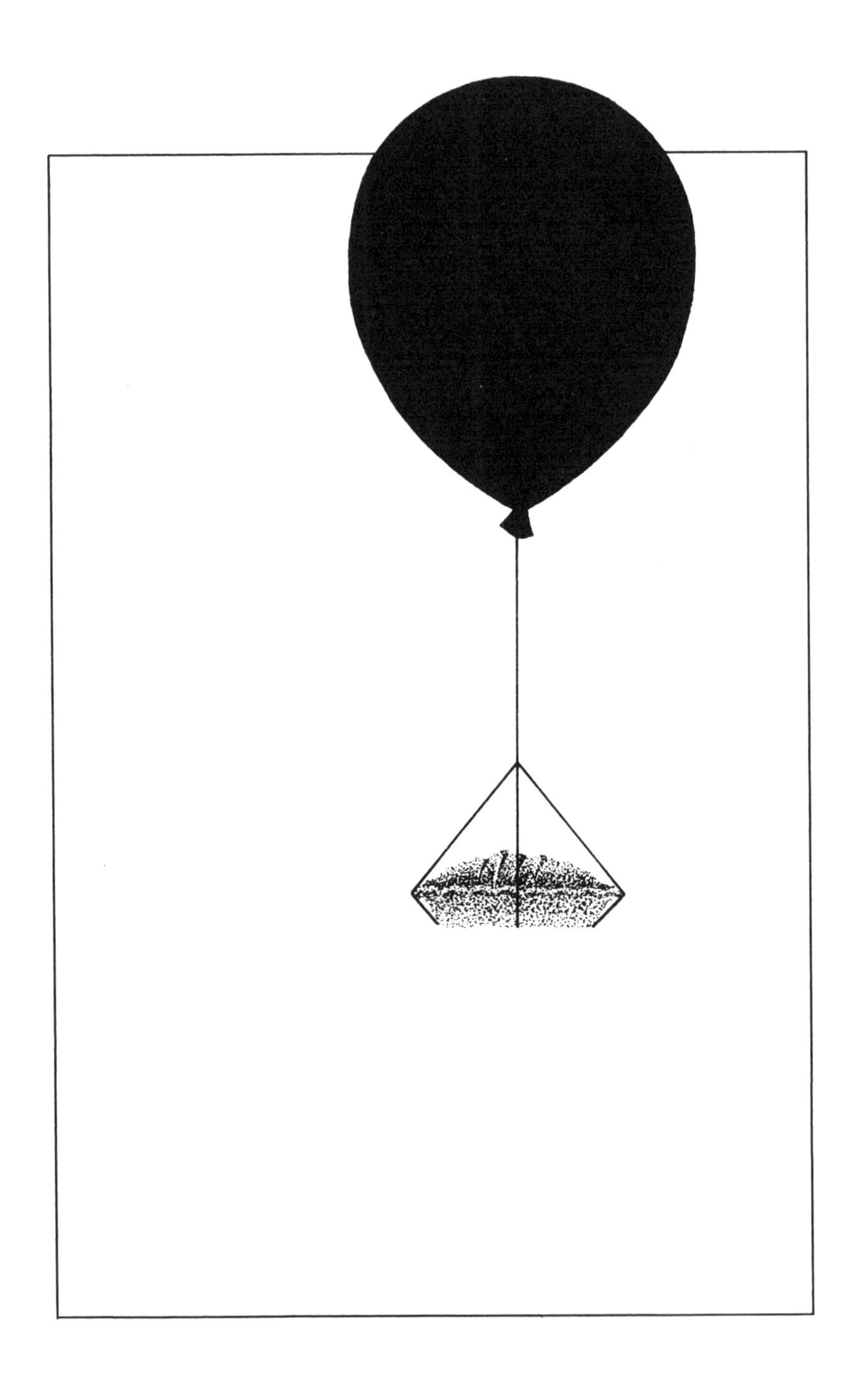

Infrared Signature

"They're doing it in Canada," he says. "I heard it on the radio. Some people up there are floating a net so they can catch a B-52." Pete's face flushes as he talks to her. He's just gotten home from work, and though his tie is off, he's still unwinding. His hands work fast, pulling a lesson planner from his stack of books and pads, grabbing a pencil from the basket on the kitchen table. "I know it'll work," he says, moving her bread racks to clear a space on the counter. "Take a look. I've already made a few diagrams."

Wheeling nods as she hears him, thinking that his drawings will be hurried and dark-lined just like his current mood. Walking past him toward the refrigerator, she slips one knuckle under the waistband of his brown corduroys, trailing it across his back as she goes to pour them both some juice. "Good day at school?" she asks, knowing that he doesn't hear her.

"It's like this, Wheeling," he says as she hands him a cool glass. "They fly trainers from Fort Mack to McQueen. My mother's seen them, once or twice a day, for years. All we have to do is make one of these things, these nets, and get it up there somehow. The rest is air currents, politics, a measure of luck."

"You want to catch a plane?"

"Yeah. Why not? Somebody's got to show these guys what they're doing." He leans back over his sheet of green-lined paper. Across the daily headings—Monday, Tuesday, Wednesday—he has sketched a pale rectangle that is anchored to the page by bright red X's and arrows he has drawn in with his grading pen. Wheeling doesn't think the net looks like much. It reminds her of the sagging contraption she and her brother would use to corral bait in the creek when they lived near the mill. The figures that Pete has arranged in columns along the margins of the diagram mean nothing to her, but she touches her finger to the sums and products he has worked out. Her hip bumps against his flat thigh as she moves closer, and she listens while Pete explains his numbers, his scope, his dimensions. His free hand rushes through his bright chestnut hair as he slides his pencil point from north to south, then east to west.

He disappears down the hall toward their bedroom just as the oven timer buzzes. Wheeling pulls the two loaves of whole wheat bread from the heat and replaces them with an apple-caramel pie she is trying for the first time. She leaves the bread on the back of the stove to cool and begins to wash the bits of clumped pastry from her hands and her fingernails, knowing that Pete must have spent his afternoon planning period reading and jotting. She can see it now. He will be up late grading homework.

She is loosening the bread from the pans and placing it on the cooling racks when Pete slides back into the kitchen in his socks. Sitting at the table with his workboots in one hand, he only glances at the envelope Wheeling has left on the red-quilted placemat before he pushes it away toward the spot reserved for guests and coupons.

"A hundred and forty-six dollars. How did we do that?"

"Oil heat and bad luck, I guess. The dream cottage here has faulty eaves. And December, up on this hill, was awful."

"Money," whispers Pete as he bends down to lace his leather boots. "We don't care about money, do we?"

Wheeling smiles and shakes her head until her long, brown hair swishes across the cream linoleum counter. Pete, she thinks, should have been an outfielder, a big band trombonist, somebody with a nice tight manager.

"That is one thing I promise you won't have to worry about with this project, Wheeling." Pete moves to the cupboard, looking for ginger snaps or sugar cookies. "It won't cost much. Not really. I've got ideas."

She watches him, considering her own budget in her head. Now that winter has really fallen in and the holidays are over, she is sure to get even more calls from the local school principals. Already, she has substituted six times in three weeks, teaching everything from remedial reading to therapeutic dance.

And there are the wedding cakes. She's recently contracted for two four-tier specials—one with a chocolate mint-flavored inside. As June approaches, well, she can smell the hurried heat of the kitchen already. If Pete will only agree to teach summer session again, she's sure they will make it fine.

"How are you going to get this net thing for cheap?" she asks, resealing the cannister of cookies he has left open.

"Easy," he says, walking across the kitchen. "Check it out."

In a minute, he emerges from the garage with his Zebco spinning rod in his hand. He lays the rod on the table and begins to fiddle with the silver-trimmed reel, all business.

"No, don't tell me that," she bursts out. "Please don't tell me that you're going to cast for a plane with fishing gear."

"Be serious," he says, turning a screw with his thumbnail until the reel is detached. "I said I'm making a net. But fishing line might be just the thing. It's light, cheap, real available. Take a look." Unthreading the line from the rod's eyes and setting the reel in the seat of a chair, Pete begins to unwind the spool. The open-face bail clicks as it spins, and Wheeling's eyes follow the rhythm of its turn as Pete's hands fill with blue-tinted line. "Ten pound test strength," he continues. "Fine for bass. Maybe not quite perfect for a jet, but it'll make my point. Two hundred and fifty yards of this stuff weighs maybe two ounces, Wheeling. And each reel filler only costs, say, five-fifty. Here, have a touch."

Wheeling holds out her small hands, and he fills them with an expanding coil of fishing line. It's light and slick like vermicelli, she thinks, only indigestible, perfectly man-made. She rocks on her heels to anchor herself when Pete begins to pull the line, yard by yard, back from her hands so he can run it between her and one of the coat hooks that is nailed next to the garage door. He loops the stuff, back and forth, until her palms are empty. Only her forearm, posed upright by Pete, remains tangled, a half-cocked counterpoint to the horseshoe coat hook. She waits patiently, hoping her free arm is within reach of the oven. As Pete begins to explain himself, Wheeling notices that her fingertips are turning white.

"Warp and woof," he says. "Sort of like this. I build a light frame, weave and balance, and launch the whole thing somehow. Probably with balloons."

"Balloons?" she asks, seeing it too quickly. Garage, kitchen, bathroom—all squeaking and rubbing with sweaty balloons.

"Yeah. Nichols gave me that idea at lunch. He has a good buddy whose into them. The big rainbow-colored jobs."

"Won't that cost something?"

"Maybe. But don't worry. I swear not to spend more than five hundred dollars."

Wheeling's ears ring a little bit with the timer. *Five hundred dollars.* She thinks she's got to talk to Pete. Sit him down. Pivoting around her well-wrapped arm, she is able to reach an oven mitt and lower the oven door. The sharp, sweet tang of the pie's heat makes her eyes water. She has removed the pie without a tilt, a burn, even a hint of trouble before Pete calls to her. She notices that her crust, hand-rolled and cut, is perfect.

You know what I like most about this thing," he shouts from the garage where she can hear him digging among his tools.

"No," she answers. "I sure don't."

"I have a feeling that my dad would have liked it," he says, coming to the kitchen door with his arms full of fishing tackle, nails, and a length of copper wire. "He would have loved a thing like this to the very end."

Wheeling is on the floor of the den pinning a shirt pattern to some striped fabric. Pete is on the phone again.

"Yeah," he says, "use the compass if you need to. And don't forget to log it. We need to cut back on the guesswork."

Wheeling figures that if she modifies the collar and cheats on the seam widths she'll have just enough cloth to make a shirt, with extra long sleeves, for Pete.

"Right," he continues, cradling the receiver against his ear while he runs a finger down what appears to be a checklist. "There's a pen inside the notebook I left on the window sill. And columns for time, direction, and estimated altitude. Uh-huh. A big help. Thanks a lot." He hangs up as Wheeling is double-checking her layout, making sure she can match stripes where she needs to. "How's your Mom?" she asks.

"Fine. Ready and willing. I figure we ought to be able to predict a steady pattern after a couple of weeks. That woman doesn't miss a trick."

Pete laughs as he settles down on the floor near Wheeling. He leaves his checklist in his lap as he sorts through the stack of books he has piled in the armchair. *World Aircraft. NATO Fighters and Attack Planes. A Pictorial History of the Flying Machine.* He flips through them all, one by one, keeping notes in a three-ring binder that he has labelled Operation Big Fish. Wheeling folds her sewing and sets it on the refinished steamer trunk they use as a coffeetable. Standing, she steps over Pete's outstretched legs and bends to lift two split oak logs from the hearth. This afternoon, it's been up to her to keep the fire going.

"Did I get the right books?" she asks, using the cast-iron poker to steady the crackling wood and establish air flow, smooth as a breeze, between the oak and some charred-down locust. "I took what I could carry."

"Well, there is a lot of Navy stuff here, and what we want is Air Force, strictly Air Force. But I think we'll be okay. My guess is that we're dealing with T-33s. Could be something newer, though. I'm tempted to call Fort Mack straight out."

"The librarian gave me everything that was in," says Wheeling. "She said that it's all very popular, very accurate material. Said that she was sure that my son would be pleased. 'Engaged, educated, and entertained' was the way she put it, I think."

"No kidding."

"My son, she said. I thought it was pretty funny."

"Most people would," Pete says, looking back down at his notes, the glossy reproductions of A-4 Skyhawks and F-16 Fighting Falcons blurring in the firelight. "I really am getting somewhere on this, though. Five thousand yards of ten pound test line ordered wholesale for a hundred bucks. And I'm thinking of taking Nichols over to Mom's Saturday morning. He flew in Korea, you know. Understands planes. If we both got a good look at one of these flights, things might really come together."

"Nichols is into this?" Wheeling asks, turning from Pete, not knowing whether to sew or cook or go into the chilly bedroom to read.

"Off and on. He likes the problem-solving part. But the actual snare? No way. He's still a poker-playing VFW on the weekends. Doesn't think I'll go through with it anyway."

"Do you really think you can yank a metal machine out of the sky?" Wheeling gathers the pinned material to her chest.

"Not yank. Just slow down. Clog. We aren't going to hurt anyone."

But he will go as far as he can. Wheeling whispers that as she stands near the doorway. "You'll go as far as you can, Pete. Right?" He doesn't hear her. He stops her only as she's walking into the kitchen where the light and surface are better for planning, piecing together.

"Hey," he says, looking up from his lap. "What are you making there?"

"A shirt," she answers. "Like the blousy one Bernard has. I'm making it from the hand-woven cotton material that Marilyn sent me from Guatemala. They're still down around there, you know. Tanner and Marilyn."

"Guatemala? Lots of trouble in Guatemala, I hear. Lots of problems."

"Yes," she says, walking on through the door.

"Who you making it for, beautiful?" he shouts, raising his voice like one of them is pulling out on a railroad car.

"I don't know," she yells back, laughing.

"Well, just don't drop the thread next time you're passing through. You can't be too careful," he joshes. "Not around here."

Sure enough, when she comes back into the den where Pete is stretched way out, smiling with his hands behind his nodding head, she sees the thread. The red spool hangs from the handle of the trunk, the thin fiber trail that she has left behind wiggling from side to side until it ends, in a curlicue, around the toe of her bedroom slipper.

When Drake calls the first time, Wheeling is careful to take a complete message. *E. Drake at 2:45,* she writes. *Will be at Billy's (665-8257) until Wednesday. Please return call.* But the second or third time, she is a little less patient. "Yes," she tells the man on the other end of the line, "I've got the message down. No, Pete's not in yet. I'm sorry." She relaxes some when the voice—a slow, deep curdle of a voice—tells her that he is an old friend, just an old high school friend, who is back in town for a while. "No big damn deal," he tells her twice. "Pete Kinston will always know where to find me."

She is still a little surprised at Pete's reaction to the messages. He has always been impatient with things like this—Washington High, balding friends, the past—before. "Ears! The Big E!" he shouts, shouldering her rolling pin like it is a bat. "Best switch hitter in the county, the whole damn state. I can't wait. We'll have him over. Talk. I haven't seen the son-of-a-bitch for years." Pete stops for a minute, squares around to bunt. "You'll like him, Wheeling," he says, swiveling his knees. "The fellow could be your kind of guy."

When he calls Drake, they agree to meet at Trout's Place for a beer or two before dinner. "On me, you bastard," Pete yells, still waving the rolling pin in one hand. "And then dinner here. With Wheeling. . . . Yeah, the one you've been talking to." Before he leaves, he kisses Wheeling on the nose, the lips, and tells her that he really hopes it won't be much trouble. "Earhart Drake is a big guy, but polite," Pete tells her. "I know he'll eat whatever's rustled up."

They are back at seven, only half an hour later than Wheeling figured, so the pot roast is not too dry and is still a big hit. Drake, though, is a little much for Wheeling to take in all at once. He's tall, even taller than Pete, and solidly built—like a brick mason or a highway construction worker, she thinks. But his long hair and untrimmed beard throw her off kilter. "I was in the military quite a while," he says as he yokes his hair in a rubber band before they sit down to eat. "But I gave it up."

All three of them stay at the table until after nine, drinking beer, talking, finishing at least two servings of roast and vegetables each. Wheeling serves her fresh yellow pound cake for dessert, but only after Drake has eaten every single potato she has cooked and has offered to wash the dishes. "Pete and I go back a long way," he says, quietly stacking the plates with his broad-fingered hands, "but I've been around, and I think I know how to handle people from outside of this county. I'm sure you and me will get along fine."

Wheeling is flattered when he asks her about her work, her teaching and her cooking. Pete's friends don't usually bother. And she is surprised how close she feels to herself when she confesses her greatest dream to him, out loud, while she is brushing crumbs from the tablecloth with the side of her hand.

"I'd like to have a bakery of my very own," she tells him. "I'd like to feed these people right." By the time they have finished cleaning the kitchen, they have touched on many things—Drake's baseball days, his stint in the Philippines, children, insulation, pike fishing at the lake. They finish their conversation by comparing shampoos and the assets of natural bristle hairbrushes, both of them drying dishes with embroidered terry cloth towels.

Pete, of course, can't wait to get Drake into the garage. "I'm honing something that's right up your alley, buddy. I want you to take a look. Wheeling can get the coffee." He waves for Drake to follow him. "E. Drake was nearly in 'Nam with the Marines," he says to Wheeling as she leans against the frame of the garage door, watching the two of them pick a path to the cluttered work table that is covered with charts and drawings. "He just missed it. I'm sure he'll have some sharp ideas."

They don't emerge until after midnight. Wheeling has changed into her striped flannel nightgown and slippers, but she is still awake, looking at a household wares catalog by the fireplace. When Pete and Drake come into the den, she notices that their eyes are very bright from excitement, maybe from the cold air of the garage. Pete hugs her, nearly lifting her off her feet, and stretches out her hand for Drake to grab onto, to shake. "We've got a genius here," Pete says, squeezing her again, her hair catching in the buttons of his shirt.

"What's the word?" Wheeling asks, holding Pete's arm around her waist. "What did you figure?"

"Well, it's like this," Pete answers. "We use a sturdy rope frame and suspend a certain amount of ballast from the bottom of the net to keep it spread. Big E here thinks balloons are okay to get us up there. The tough part will be gauging the jet's flight path, but I'm leaving that to my right arm here."

Drake smiles. "I had a good buddy in artillery," he says. "I know a few things, and I can see that baby speeding in right now." He squats as he speaks, his ponytail under his collar, his stained goose-down vest bunching up around his waist. It takes Wheeling a minute to recognize the pivoting, the squinting of the eyes, the upright grip of one fist. He is firing, Drake is following the flight of a target and firing at it right across the paneling of the den. She is surprised that there is no noise.

"The whole operation is framed in our chilled little minds," Pete says. "Beer all around."

While Pete is emptying the refrigerator, Drake stands and moves over to Wheeling, putting his left hand, the one that is spotted with grease, on her shoulder. Wheeling notices, for the first time, that his brown eyes are rimmed with gold. "I think he's trying to get the courage up to tell you something," Drake says. "But it's my thing, and I don't believe in weighing old friends down unless it's necessary, unless the whole roof is falling in. So let me tell you." He drums one of his fingertips on her collarbone. "I don't have a place to stay. Things have just slid to a stop, and I don't even have plans. Pete thinks maybe I could stay here."

Wheeling looks at him, blinks, watches as he drops his hand from her shoulder and just lets it straighten, swing. In the kitchen, Pete is making rapid-fire sounds against his teeth. "I only get carried away like I just did on occasion," he says, "and you won't have to worry about the dog being too much trouble. I only let her in after dark."

Pete and Drake spend two weeks weaving the net. Pete has to give up a Saturday afternoon to record his seventh graders' mid-quarter grades and comments, so Wheeling helps out, measuring line to Drake's specifications and handing him tools—wire cutters, clamps, a stapling gun—when he needs them. The Operation Big Fish timetable, which has been taped to the freezer door, records an estimated test launch date the first week in March. "We'll just give the whole thing a shot with the balloons, ground lines, everything going," Pete says. "We'll set our sights on the kinks. Then, we call in the media."

Even while Pete is at school, Drake spends most of his time in the garage. Wheeling lends him the clock radio from the bedroom every morning and guesses that he is happy whistling to WNLL-Pure Country as he works. She spends her mornings in the kitchen baking rolls for a neighbor's anniversary buffet and testing frosting for her butter cream Easter eggs. Because she is alone, she often lets Drake's dog, Honey, inside to lick the leftovers from the mixing bowls.

There is nowhere for Drake and Honey to stay but the den, so they stay there—Drake on the couch in his military issue sleeping bag, Honey on an old plaid armchair cushion that Drake picked up at a flea market. Drake is careful to keep his spot neat, and it is over a week before Wheeling wakes up early enough to see him so much as refluffing the pillows on the couch. In fact, Drake insists on keeping the signs of his presence to a minimum. Point blank, he asks Wheeling for only two things. "I'd like to keep my toothbrush out," he says to her as he's scrambling some eggs, "just so it doesn't start to go bad on me. And Polly's picture, too. I thought maybe I could set it up on that shelf in the bathroom, next to the little towels."

Wheeling has no objections. The picture of Polly—a tiny, dark-skinned Filipino girl who Drake says he felt like he had to leave behind—seems just right to her. It is small, clearly-focused, unsmeared. The spread of Polly's smile is perfectly colored, perfectly marked. Although the back of the photo says that she is 5′2″, 100 lbs., only seventeen years old, she looks to Wheeling like a woman who knows her man. Because the pose is sassy and one-footed, Wheeling guesses that Drake took the photo himself.

"She must have been interesting. Different," Wheeling says when Drake first sets the picture on the shelf.

"Yeah," he says. "She must have been."

Four days before the scheduled test launch, Drake tells Wheeling that he has tried to keep from feeling guilty from the beginning. "I know I'm chipping in my share of the groceries, but let me fix you lunch. I really want to keep things even between us." Thinking that he is on the road to making her nervous, she nods and lends him the car keys so he can go to the store. At one o'clock they sit down to servings of rice and vegetables covered with a spicy peanut sauce, the only Indonesian dish Drake knows how to make. "I sometimes crave things once I've left them behind," he tells her. "Over there, I ate mainly hamburgers."

Wheeling enjoys the meal and is honestly able to smile when he asks her two days later if she'd like him to make it again. "Sure," she says, "let's double it this time, though, and save some for Pete. He can take it in and heat it in the lounge microwave."

"Good idea for a good man," Drake responds, checking the carrot and celery supply in the refrigerator. "He is a good man, don't you think?"

"We've been together seventeen months."

"Yeah, I knew him when he was sticking it out with Sharon. A steady fellow. Focused. He sees right through most things."

"I like to think of him as my best friend," Wheeling says, adding onions and rice to her grocery list. "The kind of person you can team up with without getting too lost."

"Me, too," says Drake. "Polly was the same for a while. Holding her hand made me feel a little younger, a little smaller. You though," he says, wiping his mustache with his finger, "you aren't really like the ladies I go with."

Wheeling bites the tip of the pencil she's holding. "Why?" she asks. "What do you mean?"

"Wrong kind of spirit," he says. "Now don't take that hard or anything. You are a fine woman. But Pete has got the spirit I like. This project, for instance, is pure Pete. I'm just the ticking of a buried bomb. You know, part of the trigger."

"Trigger?"

"Yeah, the thing that gets him going where he wants to go. You do that for him too."

"I do?"

"Sure. He told me all about it."

Because of a problem with the balloon rental company, the test launch is cancelled. "God damn them for not being ready for good weather," Pete shouts. "People like that should never overcommit themselves."

"What do we do?" Wheeling asks.

"We go up pure and clean. Friday's test pilots run the corridor at 10:45 or so. Mom's got it all down."

"We got a way to go yet, Pete," Drake says. "Those latest ballast harnesses are shit."

"Roll up your sleeves then, Earhart. Six days and counting."

While Pete and Drake work in the evenings, Wheeling cooks, sews, and sends a few postcards to old college friends. *Wish you could see this upcountry thaw*, she writes. *Sometimes I get the feeling whole surfaces are just washing away. Pete and I are fine, and we have a dog now (sort of). See you after spring cleaning, I hope.*

Love, Wheeling. Most of the postcards are photos of hot air balloons floating through clouds or hanging, it looks like, from the flat backboard of a blue Nebraska sky. It is her private joke. I'll tell them the whole story later, she thinks. When we've made our cast.

During the days, Drake is sure that he wants to work alone so Wheeling goes into town to place advertisements for her wedding cakes and other fine baked goods. Twice, she goes to the library—first, to return the books she has taken out for Pete; later, to do some reading on her own. The plan to throw a net, the nearly weightless bulk of an idea, into the air has grown on her, but she is a little unsure of the consequences, the possibility of its success. She is comforted to find that the low, wide reading tables of the library give her hope, access to facts, a sense of ease. Scanning the back issues of newspapers and becoming familiar with big names in big professions pleases her. It is like being back in college where people move, try things, shout ideas into a kind of friendly emptiness. She is glad to know that people are still trying things, and she can't wait to tell Pete what she has found out. Not because he will care but because it will give him something to work against.

"I read up on that Canadian net," she says when all three of them are eating dinner. "I found articles in the Winnipeg Free Press. The B-52 they went after was flying by radar. It was being guided by the cruise missiles it was carrying, and the guys inside, the crew, weren't in control." She passes Drake the biscuits. "The net still missed, though."

"I knew that from day one," Pete says, his mouth full of spinach. "It's the idea that I liked."

"Won't really matter if our pilot can manuever or not," Drake adds. "He isn't going to be able to see what he's dodging."

"Except for the balloons," Pete reminds him.

"Those balloons will look like shadows on his radar screen."

"That peace group is going to keep trying," Wheeling tells them. "Every time the Air Force runs a test. The activists are prepared to accept full responsibility."

"So am I," Pete says, reaching for more chicken. "Drake and I both. Too bad the military doesn't think the same way."

During dessert, while she is dolloping freshly whipped cream on the servings of blueberry cobbler, Wheeling tells them about how she's been getting the big picture. "I spent a whole afternoon with just the *Scientific Americans*," she says. "Incredible."

Pete says that he had enough of that in college. Drake says that after years in the service, well, he knows what he needs to know about these things.

"But perspectives change," Wheeling insists. "It all looks different every day you get older and every time one of the angles in your life shifts. Taking a look really helped me," she says, staring at them both until they drop their forks against their dessert plates. "I feel like I have the perspective of one those satellites now. Not real clear yet, but broad, full range."

The two men, Pete and Drake, take their own dishes to the sink and head for the garage. Wheeling follows them.

"I just want you two to know that I'm in on this," she says softly. "I understand. But I can't really handle shots in the dark." She spreads her arms wide, for just a second. "It's like this satellite thing. The advanced ones, the killers, they have these lasers that can detect the heat quotient of missile boosters and tell one kind of Russian missile from another. They read the signatures—the infrared signatures, they're called—and zero in. One little machine finds another in all that atmosphere, all that space."

"And then ZAP," laughs Drake. "Nuked out."

Wheeling doesn't look at him. "That's not what I mean."

"What are you trying to tell us?" Pete asks.

"That I'm with you, but that I think something's missing."

"Huh?"

"The Canadians, they had a sign. They had words for what they were up to."

"So?" Pete asks, leaning over the checklist that is on his worktable.

"So, I thought you ought to have this. Like the Canadians up there," she says, taking a grocery bag from her sewing table and handing it to Drake who is closest to the door. Drake looks at the bag, which is light and stuffed full of fabric, but he doesn't touch the contents. Wheeling can see that he is trying not to smile, that he is trying not to say Oh, thank you, bright infrared is my favorite color.

Wheeling helps Pete pull the nightgown over her head as she straddles him. But she lets him settle her hips in his hands, knowing that she will be amazed at his touch which is thorough, complete, which always begins, like a brushstroke, at her shoulder blades. She watches him as she feels his fingers, looking above his jutting chin at his still mouth, his nose. She wishes she could see in the night; she wishes she could sight the pinpoints of his eyes. He shifts her a little to the left and pushes against her when he is ready.

And he is the one who stops. He moves his hands from her ribs to the long hair that rustles against her arms. "You're still thinking about the project, aren't you?" he says.

"I guess so. I just wanted to help out," she says. "I'm never comfortable when you go it alone."

Pete drops his hand to his chest. "I *am* nervous about it," he says. "My heart is banging."

"But you think I'm silly, don't you? Out there. Off in space."

"No, you're just coming in from your own spot."

"It means a lot to you. I know that."

"Yeah, but I don't even know if I'm sure what the stakes are."

"The stakes could be this," Wheeling says, lowering herself until her hair is like a swaying tent around their faces. "I need you, I care for you. Some things never change."

She says nothing more, only sighs when Pete finds her again in the dark. He can be so good at it. Out in the den, Honey whimpers like she's calling to a dream. In seconds, it seems to Wheeling, the dog is echoed by Pete, who gives his response with a nod and a gasp. Somewhere in those sounds are codes Wheeling is sure she can break. She listens, listens until her ears ring, as Pete rolls to his side of the bed. "I love you, too," she finally says, slipping under the sheets to sleep by his side.

Pete calls in sick the day of the launch. "It's my throat," he tells the principal's secretary. "So sore you wouldn't believe it." Wheeling has filled the thermos with coffee and packed the cinnamon buns by the time he is off the phone. The truck is loaded, and the balloons, two of them, are already out at the farm. Nichols and his buddy delivered them after work on Thursday. Pete's mother has called about them twice. "Can't believe it," she tells Wheeling. "They're just beautiful."

Pete, Drake, and Wheeling ride together in the front of the truck. There is just enough room for Honey to stay in the back with the net. "Toyota," Drake shouts as he slams the door, shutting them all in together. "They make a great little truck."

Pete laughs. "Ingenuity," he says. "It's the name of the game."

Everybody feels like singing during the ten-minute drive to the farm, but they can't agree on a radio station. Drake settles the matter by turning the radio off and conjuring up a medley which includes the Washington High fight song and a few old boot camp chants. Wheeling and Pete join in when he gets to "God Bless America." As they sing, the windshield is frosted with their breath.

Nichols and the balloons' owner have promised only one thing. That the balloons—small, helium-filled models—will be ready to go at nine o'clock. So Pete drives straight to the calving barn in the northern pasture where, sure enough, two blue-striped globes are waiting, rocking in the breeze. Nichols and his buddy, who stayed with the balloons most of the night, are nowhere to be seen. "My man wants one hell of an alibi today," Pete says, as he parks the truck by an old cattle chute. "So he's drinking coffee with Miss MacGregor right this minute. Admiring her tits."

"Good job, though," Drake says, shading his eyes as he looks up at the balloons. "You and I will be able to handle these babies, no problem."

While Pete and Drake lower the tailgate, Wheeling sets the thermos on the hood of the truck and double-checks the binoculars. After the net is unrolled, clipped in, and secured, it will be her job to sight the target. She is nervous. She has read in two different places that jets can travel at up to 900 miles per hour. She is sure that she will see nothing.

The first balloon has been attached and Pete is busy untangling the right edge of the net when Honey barks and heads through the mud toward a yellow-clad figure walking up the hill.

"Security alert," says Drake, stuffing his ponytail under his Orioles cap. "Let's keep our story straight."

But Pete doesn't even bother to turn around. "It's my Mom," he says. "She'd never miss this. I'd guess she's got her camera."

Sure enough, Marjorie Kinston, wearing her dead husband's slicker and boots, starts clicking away with her Nikon as soon as she catches her breath. "Look around here, Earhart," she says while Drake is arranging the ground lines. "I remember you from fifth grade on." She takes a picture of Wheeling, too, as Wheeling is pointing the binoculars into the cool sun like she's searching, looking hard for something. "You're a beautiful girl, honey," she says. "That's going to come out great with the sun splashing off those lenses like that."

By ten o'clock they are ready for lift off. Wheeling straddles the fence and releases the balloons. As they rise, the ground lines that are held by Pete and Drake snap with tension. The net sags for a minute then fills out, billowing like it's underwater. Stretched like a veil or a sun-dried web, it can hardly be seen against the sky. Only the lower left hand corner flaps with visibility. There, Wheeling's letters have been loosely stapled to the woven fishing line.

"Not bad," Pete's mother says, waving goodbye as the jumble of rope and plastic rustles above her head. "S-T-O-P. I should have taken your picture next to that."

"I would have done more," says Wheeling, her hands deep in her coat pockets. "But I ran out of material."

At 10:15 they are set, resting steadily at six hundred feet. Pete's mother is helping Drake keep his lines untangled, laughing because he checks the wind with his wet thumb every two minutes. She tells him that she's got these Air Force boys figured. "I feel I know each one by the way he crests my ridge here," she says.

Drake agrees. "The Air Force," he says, "never does anything you can't predict. We used to kick their butts. In training, womanizing, softball, everything. Especially softball."

Wheeling stays close to Pete in case he wants help. But he doesn't say much, both hands tight on the ropes. His eyes scan the clearing horizon for something he knows he will have to see because, as he tells Wheeling, at this speed, your sight is all you have. "I'll cut this rig loose if I have to," he says. "Just to have a chance." He urges Drake to go all out and release the slack. "Let's string to seven hundred and twenty-five. I want those suckers up there."

At 10:45, Earhart Drake is describing Polly to Pete's mother, saying yes, she's about your height, and sure enough, you have her eyes. Or near enough. That brown you've got in there is remarkable. At 10:47, Pete and Wheeling see it, almost at the same second, cutting through the washed out sky like a blade.

"God damn, god damn, god damn," Pete shouts. "Let her rip."

"Up, up," yells Wheeling. "We've got to get up."

In a split, Drake has followed Pete's lead and opened his hands to the whirring of the rope. The balloons lunge into an updraft, but it is too late. The jet tilts off to the west, slick as a silver-tipped dart. The only thing they catch is a rumble which shivers in Wheeling's ears like it shivers across the skin of the balloons that are rising, rising into the air.

"Adjust one degree south, point two-five KM altitude," says Drake, his fist over his mouth like he's holding a radio mike. "We just missed the bastard."

"Well, that one," says Marjorie Kinston with her camera to her eye, "had a number 3 on its tail. And a 7. Saw them plain as day. Just like the ones last week."

Wheeling doesn't say anything. She just stands in the muddy tracks of the truck with the binoculars around her neck, expecting Pete, who she can see out of the corner of her eye, to explode. She'd like to try it all again, get it right this time. She'd like a little practice. We can only get better, she thinks, as she begins to walk toward Pete to comfort him, the wet clay sucking at her boots.

But when she gets close to him, close enough to smell the dusty corduroy of his jacket, she sees that his lips are moving calmly, opening themselves just enough to whistle with sound.

"A beautiful thing," she hears him say as he points at the balloons with two flapping hands. "The most beautiful thing I've ever seen."

"But we missed," she says. "We were way off."

"Yeah," he says. "But we're here. We went for it." He pats her on the back. "You understand. Maybe the sky's not my bag. Drake has been thinking of going into charter fishing on the lake. He asked me about it." Wheeling stares at him, the pit of her stomach going cold. "Got to wait for my rig to come down first though."

"Your rig," Wheeling shouts, feeling her forearms tingle. "That mess belongs to all of us. You can't act like it's your personal toy."

"Hey, take it easy, Wheels," Drake says, coming toward her. "We aren't in the bottom of the ninth here."

She doesn't even take a breath. "All I need are the keys," she says, her hands clenched on the binoculars. "I'm going after that thing right now."

After she takes the keys from Drake, Wheeling walks to the truck as slowly as she can manage. She can't believe that they've just fired one big blank. Pete's mother starts to intercept her but thinks better of it. Only Honey gets near enough to touch her, to feel the warm tremble of her hand. As she pumps the engine to a roar, Drake yells that the balloons are heading west and that they should drop in an hour or two.

"Good," she yells back. "I hope to God the whole thing lands right in the middle of everybody's life. A huge fucking raft of spirit."

She backs out of the barn lot and shifts into the gear that will take her right across the morning. She's on her way downhill, the tailgate rattling, when she hears a shout and checks her mirror to see Pete leaping after her, his jacket flapping against his ribs.

"Hey, hey," he calls. "Wait a minute."

Before her, through the curved windshield, Wheeling sees the blue-striped pair of balloons turn slowly like eggbeaters or whirlygigs or professional dance partners. She brakes. In a second, the truck door opens, and Pete takes the binoculars off the seat where Wheeling has left them. "I could ride shotgun here," he says, looking at her, his hand patting the black vinyl seat cover. "Handle the radio."

"Stick it out with Drake," she says, taking her foot off the brake so that the truck rolls forward a few inches. "I'll call you when I need you."

Pete leans inside the truck until she can feel his breath in her ear. He reaches for her shoulder. "Drake's got business here," he says quietly, pointing a thumb up the hill. "As you said, you and I've got contraptions to track down."

Wheeling drops her forehead onto the cold plastic of the steering wheel. Pete is a slash of auburn, a discernible column of light in the corner of her eye. She can touch him with her elbow if she tries. Inhaling the stale air of the truck, she realizes that all she wants to remember right now is the thrill of the launch. The cleanup, the mistakes of the flight can come later. "Only if I drive," she says, lifting her face toward the roof.

"Okay, my gal. Cool."

She shifts the truck into neutral letting it drift toward the gate on its own. Behind them, Pete's mother is posing Drake and Honey for photos, the dog in Drake's arms, the yellow slicker hanging by its hood from his head. By the time the Toyota has reached the road, Wheeling notices that Mrs. Kinston has redirected her camera, and it is, Wheeling thinks, aimed at the truck. The truck where maps unfold across the dashboard.

Stadia

Laura did what he would have done if he had been in control of himself. She bought five, or was it six, pairs of tickets to Tiger ballgames, she filled her gas tank, and she waited. She knew he was too stubborn to break on the actual anniversary; Dan would never admit to that kind of memory. But he would weaken. Light rain, the rattle of a passing dump truck, LIVE BAIT signs would bring him down. She had only to watch his face instead of the numbers. May 3rd, May 4th, the double-header on the 9th: she had tickets for them all.

Dan's father had died a year earlier, before Laura met Dan at the MacNeil's dinner party. The illness, she understood, had been long, lingering—a thing with no boundaries. The last few weeks had dwindled on in the hospital. For Laura, the very thought of a fading death, a death without cutting shock, was numbing. Because there was no way to mark the thing then, to feel the edges and have done with it. And, for her, the power of love and grief was precise and exacting. She remembered exactly how and why she had fallen in love with Dan. His confusion with the formal silverware. His nervous finger tracing the pattern on the handle of the salad fork. That picture was frozen. So was her knowledge of Dan's father. Liver and kidney failure. Cirrhosis. A funeral in the rain and the small photo on the shelf at Dan's old house. She had put together a thin collage of what she thought and what she'd heard, and it held. But for Dan she supposed it wasn't so easy. He didn't build his scenes, so the stray pieces, floating loose around him, got to him all the time. Laura knew that. Because when he saw a State Road crew on the highway or heard his father's old fly rods fall off their rack in the garage, his hands shivered over whatever they were trying to grasp.

Laura also knew she couldn't quite fix it for him. They had lived together for six months, but his father was his past. She could only buy the tickets, get him into Detroit, mix him with a crowd. And she was sure she would have to play it gracefully, like every move was pure instinct, as if they always lived like that—on tour, driving for pleasure. She couldn't let him know what she was up to, how she was moving them both forward, or he would balk. "This kind of thing has got no anniversary, no God damn memory," he'd say. "It just happens."

So she kept the tickets in her jewelry box, a place he never looked, and they were the first thing she touched, really touched, when she finished her shift at the bookstore. They lay on top of her passport in a paper clip, looking like bookmarks that needed to be handed out and given their place in the world. The enameled bracelets she rarely wore, the oddly-shaped earrings that lay nearby in their own velvet-lined compartments were just accessories, dull accomplices, in comparison. They clacked when they moved. Laura found their jumble irritating in the afternoons, and she passed over them. Instead, she touched the quiet tickets with fingers that smelled of the Windex she used to polish the store windows. She unclipped them, counted them, rearranged them with the current pair on top. Often, she found herself acutely aware of the way her damp skin smeared the glossy surface of the heavy, thick-edged paper.

Laura knew several people—Crista, Hank, even the Levys—who would have been glad to take the unused tickets on short notice. But she called no one. The seats were good seats along the third base line, Dan's kind of seats, and she wanted them to be empty and waiting. Waiting for Dan's distraction. Fanning the tickets across her palm, she occasionally considered memorizing their numbers so that she, and only she, would know where to place herself and Dan when the time came. But when she thought about it, the gesture seemed extravagant, a little cold and thin, even to her. The tickets already told her where to enter, when to arrive, how to find their spot. That, she considered, was probably enough.

The truth of the matter was that Dan's father had never taken his son to a ballgame. Though the two of them had fished Four-Mile Lake, the Huron, and even the Maumee River, with a transistor radio next to their tackleboxes, they had never seen a game in Tiger Stadium. Not together. Dan had sometimes driven to Detroit in his father's truck with his friends crowding the cab that was littered with screwdrivers and bits of twisted wire. But his father never went along. "I've been on those roads all my life, practically built the ramps on I-94 by myself," he'd say, "I'd rather stay at home, listen to the game on the porch." That was the way Dan remembered it, the way he told it to Laura with his hand rubbing the back of his neck. His father couldn't stand to be crowded. Which was why the man was always at the head of his road crew, double-checking the surveyor's stakes and setting the MEN AT WORK signs just the way he liked them. Which was why the hospital finally killed him. He was, Dan said, a man who'd rather see roads and games and the slight paths of fish form in his mind. He had no use for stadiums. "He'd set up an outfield wherever we were," Dan told Laura. "Maples in left, laurel in right, the river as the foul line. And we'd see the whole thing happen right before us. Of course, he was way off. Ballfields are a lot smaller than you think, really. But we loved it. Fishing, listening, the sky folding down over the river."

But Laura couldn't take Dan fishing. It wasn't her territory. And it would just suck Dan in—the thick smells, the whiz of reels, the way the heat broke across the water. His eyes, amber eyes, would flatten with a tensile strength that he convinced himself he had, and he'd start to drink. A few beers, a shot of whiskey—his own brand, never his father's—while he looked through the trees toward as much open air as he could sight. Laura was sure that would happen. She'd seen it before. At Thanksgiving, when Dan hadn't been able to get his father's truck started, he had disappeared for hours only to return in the middle of the dinner his mother had cooked, swearing and laughing because the Bears had killed the Lions, and he had lost $20 on a bet. His eyes were watery and tarnished, his breath too sweet to be believed. Laura had sat across the dining room table from him, her eyes on her empty dinner plate. Dan's mother had just wanted the truck revved up and checked on; she was planning to lend it to her grandson in the summer. But Laura never saw Dan go near the garage again, not after he sobered up. For the rest of the holidays, he left his mother's house through the front door.

No, Laura had her room to maneuver, and she would stay on her track. She'd take him to Detroit, her town, and spin him on the hub of the city. Keep his mind off things because, well, as far as she knew, no one ever really grieved in Detroit.

For more than a week, then, she called him from the store every morning, between customers. "How are you? What's happening?" she'd ask, covering her right ear so that she could hear him, clearly and carefully, on the other end of the line. She knew exactly what she was listening for. "Not much," he'd say. "Busy. And I can't wait to get home. Relax at home." She could hear him tilt back in his desk chair when he said that. "Yes," she would answer, perhaps laughing a little, breathing lightly. "I'll be there. I'll see you there." And she would hang up, planning the dinner they would cook together in her mind. Bright fruits and vegetables. Chicken or fresh seafood. Dan's white shirt sleeves rolled above his elbows and swaying. The way she saw it, everything came together, stayed together.

Still, the emptiness drifted in like a drought, slow and irritating, and she felt it. Dan began to spend more time alone, walking along the edges of the yard behind the house as the sun set. He ate less, staying up well into the night watching television. When he touched her, his fingers didn't move. And it seemed to Laura that he always had a beer in his hand. He never said anything—not about his father, not about what it felt like to be alone in that way. But when his mother or sisters called, he was short, almost rude, handing the phone to Laura as soon as he possibly could. Sometimes, he would get out of bed just before dawn and move around the house with the lights off. Laura could hear him digging through boxes in the study or rearranging tools in the garage. In the morning, she found things, leftovers. An old pipe that had been half-heartedly smoked. A set of unmatched screws on the kitchen table. And always, she could follow the wandering trail of juice glasses sticky with whiskey or the abandoned foam of a beer to every corner of the house.

Finally, he was hardest hit on a Thursday. Laura called him in the afternoon because inventory of a new shipment of paperbacks had tied up her morning. "How are you?" she asked, after getting past the secretary. "What was for lunch?"

There was a pause before Dan responded. When he did speak, his voice sounded like a leak. "Nothing, nothing much. I ate alone."

"Oh?"

"I'm working late tonight."

"Tonight?" she asked.

"I need to do things." She could see him, his tie loose, his hand over his closed eyes. She wondered if he'd already had a drink, a memory. "We don't have plans, do we?"

"Yes," she said evenly, imagining him sinking noiselessly in his chair. "A surprise. I wanted to surprise you."

"Me." It wasn't a protest, not even a question. Just a syllable, Laura thought, trying to travel.

"Uh-huh. Tickets to the Tiger game. Pierce got them for me. Why don't you have the business world hold on for a while."

He actually considered refusing her. She could tell that. All of his desire to be alone, to put on his jeans and putter like his father had was pressed into the split second of a sigh.

"We'll be behind the dugout," she offered. "They're playing Toronto."

"Okay," he said. "Okay. I'll be home early."

He cut the line before Laura could end the conversation and clear her own mind, and unspoken words continued to circle in her head like a taped loop. This is a good idea, her head told her, echoing and spinning as she went back to inventory. I know this is a good idea.

And it was a good idea. Solid and neat. It had the rough, fresh energy of renovation that the ideas she and Dan developed together always had. After all, no one else had thought to rent the shabby little cottage on 3rd street and regrade the yard so the basement no longer flooded. No one else stayed so happy in second-hand cars. Together, they had a great deal of potential. Everyone said so. But everyone—her friends, his friends, the relatives—was also quick to qualify things in a whisper. If you two keep going like you're going, they said. Make sure you don't stop, honey. Don't hold back.

To tease herself, then, Laura arranged the details of their

departure for Detroit as if she was managing a rehearsal, a run-through of something that would, and should, replay itself in their lives. She put on a pleated white skirt and a light cotton sweater that Dan had given her for her birthday. She pushed her jeans into the back of her dresser drawer and tried a little eye liner, something different, beneath her lower lashes. She made several tiny changes that Dan would never notice, moving his tie pins from the windowsill, pressing noticeable but not definite creases in his khakis. She chose his shirt, something she usually did after they made love in the morning, and she hid his favorite sweater in the study. She also left the front door open so that she could see Dan come toward her from the driveway with only the fine mesh of a screen between them, their sounds, their motions.

She met him with a kiss on the lips, ruffling his brown hair with her fingers while he stood with his hands swinging by his sides. He seemed to be looking right past her, through the kitchen and her smile, while his eyes adjusted to the cool shadows of the foyer.

"Ready to go already, huh," he said. "Nice skirt. Just give me a minute."

Watching him walk down the hall to the bedroom, her fingers twisting the ends of her long yellow hair, Laura thought that he looked tired, more tired than he had that morning. His shoes scuffed the floor; his suit jacket dangled from his hand. When he stepped into the bedroom, he did something he almost never did: he shut the door.

"I put your clothes out for you," she said, leaning down the hallway, her voice a weak buzzing in her ears.

"What?"

"Your clothes. On the bed."

"Oh, sure. Thanks."

His distance immediately made her want to lock things. The porch door, the catch on her bracelet, the kitchen windows. While he dressed, she moved around the house in a definite circle, seeing to it that every opening and entrance clicked, snapped, or slammed with its own assurance. Security. She wished several times that she could be so strong.

Dan emerged while she was turning off the radio. He was

wearing the khakis, but his shirt he had certainly found somewhere else. Not in the closet they shared. Its pale, wrinkled plaid looked familiar to Laura but not recognizable. She knew she had seen that pattern somewhere before, and she was struck by the way the gray background of the fabric sucked the color from his eyes.

"My sweater," he said. "I need my green sweater. Then we can go."

"You think you'll need something that heavy," she said.

"Yes. Yes, I do."

Laura knew exactly where the sweater was—in a blue plastic milk crate under a pair of art books, just where she had hidden it an hour earlier. It was Dan's father's sweater, a crudely knit thing made by Dan's older sister during a time when Laura imagined that the children must have eagerly offered their talents to their parents as gifts. It had been knitted and worn before the illness, before the ugly depressions and nearly random angers had strangled the family whole. Before her. And Dan wanted it now. Right now. To wear on an evening already hot and bright enough to smear the thin smile on his face.

She walked directly into the study and got the sweater for him, dug it out. Though the sharp hiss of an opening beer can hung with her while she moved, she didn't hesitate. Instead, she folded the sweater over her arm and went for the tickets, thinking that all good ideas were slightly flexible. While Dan went into the bathroom with his beer, Laura opened her jewelry box and claimed her seats. Section 218, Row A, numbers 5 and 6. The tickets, she noticed, still smelled like ink and cool office efficiency. They were clean. She removed the pair she needed and scattered the rest on the bed. Something that Dan would notice. The tickets fell and flipped like cards from a distorted deck, fluttering awkwardly and separately as she dropped them.

He stayed in the bathroom a long time, living and breathing soundlessly for all Laura could tell. She didn't mention that she had the sweater; she didn't bother to hurry him along. She just put her wallet and the game tickets in a small leather purse and placed herself on the living room couch, imagining what spring must be like in places where the flowers bloomed as early as March. If she had flowers, she thought, she'd have different colors in her life and a man who didn't suspect that her every move was made with the chilled awkwardness of a foreigner. If they had an early spring or knew the freshness of swift change, she and Dan, she thought, could put it all together. Move closer to the city, try a three-floor condo or a refurbished co-op. Change jobs. Travel sporadically and without too many plans. Instead, Dan was slowing down and set for a quick freeze, locked in a bathroom where one poorly-placed window filtered only a flat, yellow light onto the situation.

Locked in. Running her hand over the frayed edge of a cushion, Laura could only hope that he wasn't drinking, that he wasn't, in his mind, crawling through that window in the only way he thought he knew how.

Dan eventually came to her with his car keys jangling in his hand. His face was pale, but Laura had to guess that he'd been weeping the way he did—with his lips set and his tongue pulled back in his throat to choke off any sound that might dare to emerge.

"I know what you're doing," he said, dropping his keys into her lap and reaching for the sweater that lay beside her. "Mom has called me four times this week. For no reason, she said. But I know better." He turned away from Laura, leaving her to hear the tension in his voice. "Go ahead. You do your thing, I'll do mine."

"It's just a game," Laura said, trying to stand and move near him in a way that would not seem too obstinate or direct, that might somehow rustle with love. "We don't have to go."

"No," he said, looking at her with eyes that were almost gold in their pure detachment, "we don't. But we will. You drive."

Dan kept an unopened and untouched beer between his knees the first fifteen miles on the highway. Laura glanced at it, and him, wondering if he was testing himself or her. Neither of them was talking, though Dan was a constant manager of the radio so that it whined and chattered for them. Laura kept herself together by driving wholly and intently toward Detroit, never wavering, never giving quarter to the other drivers on the road. Her irritation was washed clean by the fear that barrelled in her stomach. She tried not to think about Dan's tight fist or the stain of condensation that was spreading from the beer can to his trousers to his skin.

When they got to Romulus, Dan asked Laura to pull over. "You can get off at the next exit," he said.

"Do you want to drive?" she asked, forcing her timidity down with a swallow.

"No. Just get off. I've got to piss." His voice was sharp, but uneven, wavering as if it too was being buffeted by the cross winds that swept beneath the car. He took the beer from between his legs when the Chevy began to lean into the paved ramp that had been measured and graded by his own father. The can held steady in his hand, though his arms, as Laura could tell, were loose and sprawling as if his chest had suddenly lost all muscle. "God damn it," he said, looking to the left, past her profile. "My dad used to stay in that Holiday Inn there when the days were longest in the summer. My mother visited him once, but never again. Not on the job."

Laura glanced at the pitted rectangle of the motel. "What did he do there? Stay close to work? I know he was a hard worker," she said.

"Don't even ask what he did," Dan said as they sank with the road. "He was harder than you know."

She pulled into a gas station and waited while Dan went to the Men's Room, the can of beer in his hand. Her palms and neck were damp, and she couldn't help but notice that the pleats in her skirt were wilting. Even the air, thickening as it settled into evening, seemed stale. For the next half hour, she guessed, they would do well to use the air conditioner. After all, it was one of those nights, Laura told herself, when everything needed a little regulating.

Before Dan got back into the car, he stopped for a moment and began kicking the Chevy's front tire rhythmically, deliberately. Through the windshield, Laura could see that his hands were empty.

"Trouble?" she shouted above the rush of the air conditioner.

"No," he said, opening the door and sliding into his seat in a swirl of hot air. "Tire's fine. I've just got some mud on my boots. Trying to get rid of it."

"Mud?" She knew her own feet were clean.

"Yes," he said as she began angling into a feeder lane. "I've been around in these shoes. Sometimes, you know, I do things without you and I do them all right."

Laura felt her throat spasm again. He had to tell her he was going places she'd never seen, never even been asked to visit. With her hands hard on the steering wheel, she imagined a deep, churning path that reached along a riverbank or even, perhaps, toward an overgrown grave. She tried to imagine that he found something there. "I only try to help," she said.

"It's not that you're in the way," he continued, touching her shoulder with the back of his hand while he looked at the dashboard.

They really said nothing more to each other until they exited on Trumbull Avenue. Laura drove swiftly knowing, absolutely knowing, that the stadium and the game would turn Dan around. And indeed, he seemed to be with her as they sped deep into Detroit, the city that until the last, quick moment never seemed to have a skyline. For Laura, Detroit was a maze—gray, flat, tunneled with energy, but it was a maze that could be beaten, a puzzle that always sent her home tired and free. And Dan, Laura could see, was temporarily mesmerized by the swallow of the highways. He looked unblinkingly through the windshield, his lips moving as he read the road signs. He even seemed, from the corner of her eye, to be smiling when they finally rose off the freeway.

"Wayne State," Laura said, looking through the clean geometry of the campus toward the Renaissance Center, downtown, the dirty hints of the river. "Open campus, open stadium. Not what we're looking for tonight."

"Well, maybe not," Dan said. "But my cousin went there. He liked it."

After turning onto Trumbull, Laura let the car drift toward Tiger Stadium. They were later than she meant for them to be, and the avenue was already a crawl of vehicles. But movement was collective, not frenetic, and it was clear to Laura that she and Dan were on the verge of being gathered up in the flow of a crowd. There was comfort in that realization. From inside the Chevy, where the air was cool and motored, waving hands and flashing turn signals joined in a sort of blurred rhythm. No need for acceleration. No need for brakes. Everything just drew itself into the setting sun and the riveted gleam of the stadium.

She was surprised then when Dan asked her to pull over in front of one of the local package stores. They were almost where they needed to be, after all. Dusty kids in reflective vests swung red flags and hawked parking spots at their windshield and rear bumper. Two dollars, just two dollars—they shouted. Laura couldn't believe Dan wanted to stop now, not so close, not right there. But he was urgent, nearly angry, in his insistence. "I want some cigarettes," he said, opening his door before the car had completely stopped. "I really need them. I'll be back in a split."

The store was stained and sagging, a smeared glass front tacked to the façade of an old rooming house. Three men, the color of the fire-smoked brick walls, loitered near the reinforced doorway, shouting at friends, at fans, at anybody who drove by and was looking to talk to the streets. They drank from a dented milk jug. Laura turned away from the commotion, staring down the wide avenue that was banked by the three-story homes that had survived time and the riots. She realized, almost absently, that she had imagined orchestrating things and saving Dan in silence, well within the quiet of her mind. But out here, she and Dan were in a broader world; other people, other events were marching in to interfere. Years ago she had walked down these sidewalks with her mother and father, counting churches and the trimmed gables on the houses that seemed as large as her suburban school. Her parents had been tall and brightly-colored; her father had always had his baseball mitt. But that was before the neighborhood burned, before her father took them all right to the stadium gates in a taxi. She wished, now, that she could steer Dan like that—right through the destruction. When the men beside the car laughed loudly, slapping the crumbling pavement with their feet, she resolved to look at them and to keep looking until Dan emerged, striding in a way that only she would recognize. Because, even in this place, she was still the one who knew the way he moved.

He got into the car with an unlit cigarette between his fingers. Nothing else. No six pack, no cheap glass bottles. Laura watched him settle into his seat, noticing that he looked relaxed and perhaps a bit excited. His lips were pursed like they usually were just before he kissed her.

"Quite a place in there," he said, actually laughing as he hooked his seatbelt and she started the engine. "I think I'll prefer the ball field."

"Risky?" she asked, edging onto the street and realizing that for the first time that evening Dan was leaning out his window and helping her with the traffic.

"No, not really. It just brings back some old times. My friends and I used to stop in there."

Laura nodded.

"It's like this shirt," he said, signaling to a stringy-haired parking attendant that yes, they'd like the first and best spot they could get. "When my dad wore this shirt, well, it was movie night or visiting night or just time to get out. I'll always remember that."

"That shirt's your father's?"

"Sure," Dan said, looking down into the fabric pattern that was nearly invisible from wear. "Can't you tell. I mean I realize it's hard for you and Mom to believe, but I can handle his being gone. He was a great guy. He had his rituals." Dan got out of the car and talked to her over the dusty metal curve of the roof. "And I have mine."

They held hands as they walked toward the stadium. Dan's palm was warm and confident, and Laura decided, as she often did, that they were a pair in step. Heavy women and slender black boys enameled with sweat tried to sell them everything—peanuts, banners, decals, buttons the size of fists—but they weren't buying. Only looking, smelling, and, thank God, smiling their way through the habitual litter of a home stand. When they were in the shadows of the grandstand, Laura moved a little ahead of Dan, aiming for Gate 4 with her tickets straight and stiff in her fingers. The stadium's new shell of aluminum siding rose above her—white, grooved, resistant.

It never occurred to her that Dan was walking carefully, that his approach to the gates was consciously measured. Laura was through the chipped blue turnstile with a click, the pair of tickets torn by a man whose thumbs were red with friction. She heard bats, saw the even green of the field before she noticed that Dan wasn't with her. She turned. Behind her, people spun away from the gates like shot marbles. Behind them, Dan was being eased against a wire mesh barrier by two security guards.

His face and hands were angry. Laura could see that, even from her distance. Dan talked, he gestured sharply while a tall man in uniform searched him, then searched him again. What did he have? Laura didn't know. They hadn't arrived with anything, anything at all, except their tickets.

But it was there. A pint bottle the gleaming color of Dan's eyes, resting on the second guard's clipboard. It had been found, Laura could now tell, in Dan's boot. One pant leg was folded slightly, and his boot laces were loose and tangled. Laura froze. The pleats of her skirt swung hard against her legs. She had come in too soon. She had let Dan—lost and daring in what he remembered—get behind her.

"Nice try, fella. Nice try." Is that what they were saying to him? Laura made herself step forward.

"Take it easy. You don't understand," Dan said. "It's only a pint."

Laura could hear the pure, solitary rage in Dan's voice. It grated against the steel supports that were between them.

"I know all about it, buddy," the guard with the clipboard said as he gestured to his partner to escort Dan to the street.

"No," said Dan, as he shook the men off with a fierceness that Laura had never been sure he was capable of. "You don't understand." And he looked at her as they tried to shift him, pulling at his sweater, tearing at the collar of his shirt. He looked at her while he stood planted in a way that made him seem older and more completely trapped than he was. As old as the ground of his memories, Laura thought. As trapped as the cold metal fence that cut her sight of him into colorless pieces.

Shoreline

Nicki kissed him, quietly and softly, when they finally got ashore. The sun had set, and the deep, haunting calls of feeding loons echoed through the dark blue sky. They were late, they trailed the sunlight because it had taken so long to find the landing and register the car with the Park Service. They'd barely had enough time to paddle away from the splash of wading children and the aluminum slap of moored row boats against the water. Now, while Colin was stowing the stained orange life jackets under the canoe's seats, Nicki bent over and kissed him where his hair was long and damp. He didn't move while she ran her tongue lightly along his skin, resting it near the small mole under his left ear. She resisted the temptation to grab his flesh with her teeth.

"It will be beautiful out here," she said, stepping to the bright edge of moonlit water before he could move away from her.

"I only wish we were miles from everyone else," he said, drawing the canoe up from the lake. "Miles and miles. It's late and it's beautiful. I just want to be far away."

"We are far away," she said. "There's a lot behind us. Your laboratory. Our lease. The pictures for the layout I'm supposed to send to Quin."

"Yes, but the food and the tent are still with us," he said, slinging his pack over one shoulder. "We have work to do, Nicki, so let's try to build a fire before I fall over."

"Okay, but I'll be all right without the tent tonight, Col. We both will, won't we?"

"Yes . . . yes. I don't think it will be too cold with our equipment."

"And it will be romantic, won't it? Just you and me and the loons?"

He laughed carefully as he leaned his pack against a tree and pulled a light sweater from beneath his folded poncho. "Listen to them, Nicki. You'll have to learn what they're saying. That pair to the south has been crying in distress since we pulled in."

They both stood still for a moment, hearing the long, plaintive cries of the birds they couldn't see in the dark. She tried to pick it out. She tried to translate the fear that faded across the water as Colin put his sweater on, turned, and walked under the trees. "Come on," he finally said. "We really do have to hide the food from the bears."

Nicki gathered twigs and kindling without a flashlight. She dragged her thin fingers along the ground beneath the cool ferns growing among the maples and oaks. Branch by branch, she felt for wood, found it, and broke it while her palms became covered with wet, crumbling bark. Colin had the flashlight in a tree where he was securing their supplies with a coil of nylon cord that whistled as he drew it across the leather of his work gloves.

"Nicki," he called down after he'd tested his first knot, "I know I don't say this very much. But I can see you just beyond the firelight. You're beautiful . . . you really are."

When she looked up at him to smile from where she sat among tree roots, snapping dry sticks across her thighs, she was blinded by the white beam clenched between his legs.

"Thank you," she said.

Colin slept in his red cotton turtleneck, breathing gently, while Nicki watched the Pleiades for a falling star. Cool air came in from across the lake—she felt it on her face—and blew the coals of the fire from gray to white, lifting spark and ash into the boots left nearby to dry. Nicki had slipped into the joined sleeping bags wearing her white cotton socks and a chamois shirt. She had thrown her bra into the ferns thinking that it wasn't right, that they should be out there in the black water matched in an embrace—his large hands bearing her weight and aligning her hips; her arms, wet and slippery, locked around his neck. Instead, she was lying still, very still along the length of his bare leg, remembering what it had just been like to crawl onto his broad back and press her fingers deep into his skin, to run them along his muscles until he squeezed her hand and went to sleep. She wanted, very much, to touch him again in the darkness while she could smell him, warm and salty, on the wind. But her hands remained open and flat, her fingers tingling under her head, as she looked into the sky because she couldn't be sure he wouldn't feel it, that he wouldn't know.

"Are you thinking about him again?" she asked aloud, hearing her words stretch across the moving air. "Are you thinking of Peter? Are you dreaming about him?" She turned her head and whispered over his covered shoulder, the fingers of her left hand just brushing the ends of his hair. "I'd like to know," she said, "I'd really like to know, Colin, how much of a chance I've got."

Two days passed before Nicki had the courage to take her shirt off. When she finally asked him, the sun was high and warm on their moving, sweating backs. Colin paddled steadily in the bow, the strap of their only pair of binoculars pressing a ridge into his smooth brown skin. They had seen no one since they had sighted a beached canoe just east of Adler's Point. They expected to be alone. The rising flap of ducks or geese, their long necks stretched toward the trees, was the only sound that reached across the water.

"Col, you won't mind if I take my shirt off, will you? I'm really hot."

He chuckled under his breath. "No, the moose and I won't mind," he said. "Why should we mind?"

"Brazen, maybe," she said. "But the world seems so clear and open here."

The light wind soon dried her hot, white skin. And she felt that her steering strokes were stronger, free of the chafe of her thick cotton shirt. She blushed when Colin glanced over his shoulder once to look at her bare breasts with his steady blue eyes, and she wished she hadn't. He knew her. Only a week ago he had undressed her and laid her down beside him on the bedroom rug. Every time they passed a smooth, open crescent of sand she wanted to remind him of that. But as he said nothing, his paddle grabbing at the flat, black water before them, she thought again how it was all new and old between them. Brothers, she told herself, right now you are simply half-naked brothers on the water.

They decided to set up a three day camp at McKilnock's. The peninsula was wide and free of undergrowth, and its tip was trimmed with a short train of smooth white boulders.

"Bathing rocks," Nicki shouted as they coasted toward the shore. "You and your manuals and reports will never get me off them." She imagined herself diving over him and his papers and the clutter of camp into a clear, cold cradle of water.

"But what about my lunch?" he asked, splashing her with his trailing paddle. "What about my dinner? The dishes?"

"All yours. I'm going to get brown and eat nothing but berries right on top of that big one. And swim. I'm going to swim like a trout, like a bass."

"So, it'll be just me, all alone on shore?"

"You could always drop by. Leave your card."

"Okay then, I might," he said, tweaking her soft nipple with a calloused thumb as he helped her from the canoe. She turned, a little embarrassed, and laid her paddle in the coarse brown sand. As they unloaded the canoe, she felt him look at her when she raised her arms to pull her hair into a ponytail, when she bent over to free the bag of tent stakes from beneath the seat.

They had the tent up and a pile of wood gathered before noon. Nicki patiently scrambled eggs over the tiny Swiss stove while Colin strung up a line for damp clothes and their dew-touched sleeping bags. They ate quietly, sharing a mug of coffee and listening carefully for unfamiliar bird calls. When they finished eating the biscuits they had baked on the end of a freshly-cut stick, Colin volunteered to clean up.

"Go on. Gather some roots and berries, wild one. I'll cover this before I start working on my notes."

"Thanks," she said, squinting into the sun as she watched a small flock of swallows dip and dart overhead. "But I think I should get some more water before I play. Plenty of time to play yet. Days and days of time, right?"

She gathered the plastic bottles and an empty canteen in her arms for the trip out to the fresh center of the lake. Everything seemed broad and silent beneath the sunlight. Only he, his busy hands moving from plates to pans to the thickness of his dark brown hair, seemed different to her. How had he said it to her? Nicki, there's a new physiologist in the lab, but it's okay, okay. Nicki, there's a new slender, dark-skinned, black-eyed physiologist in my lab, on my team, but it's okay.

After she threw the containers into the canoe, she pulled off her shorts, her underwear, her watch, and pushed off for open water without looking back at Colin who was kneeling in the shadows of the camp. A new wind slid along her hips; her dark nipples tightened in the brief chill. She wondered if he was watching now. He had been standing behind her looking, she thought, at the rise of her shoulders when she had met Peter in the cafeteria, when she had shaken Salaam's hand at the department picnic.

Peter. Salaam. Chung Lee. Andrew. John. They were all kept in the back of her mind, sometimes dissolved into safety. In an ugly way, she had narrowed her eyes at each of them and had pointedly watched them walk, concentrated on the way they used their hands or opened their lips before they spoke. She had wanted to criticize their naked bodies. Just so she could continue to cluster the moments, the distinctly cut minutes, when she knew she could never walk away from Colin because she had their children, their home, their garden laid out in her mind. But the clusters were seasonal. She knew that. They went to seed, broke apart, lay—hull and kernel—in their four separate hands. As she paddled into the low waves of light she thought she should be fetching the water by swimming silently and nakedly from shore with the cold metal handle of a bucket in her teeth. Then, when she turned back for land, Colin would be a blurred stroke of motion just in sight of her water-filled eyes. He could run. She wouldn't be able to cut the weight of the lake with her arms. It would be over.

She spent the afternoon sunning herself on the rocks. While Colin read and studied beneath a tall pine tree near the shore, she swam quietly or lay upon her back with her arms flung wide as her golden hair dried between the warmth of the stone and the sun. She talked to Colin in her mind while her eyes were closed, pretending that he was leaning over her, leaning so close to her that she could feel changes in the speed of his breath. Just tell me one more time how it's true, she said, how you've never touched one of them, how you've never even talked about it aloud outside the bedroom we share. Let me hear how hard it is for you sometimes, even while you're saying you love me, to get yourself past the way he tosses his head while he talks or smiles when he's bending over the microscope. I just need to hear it again, Colin, she thought. It'll keep me from doing things, from saying to you that my belly will stretch awfully and beautifully when I'm pregnant and that I can't wait till it's that way.

With her lips just barely moving, she watched Colin draw near to take her picture while he thought she was asleep with her wet hair tangled wildly across her breasts. She knew he thought everything had just fallen that way. He thought she could just lie there distantly beautiful and move him to try to draw her with long, curved pen strokes in the margin of his notebook. She saw him, through a half-open eye, focus steadily on her slim, silent body, the camera masking his face as it clicked and whirred. Colin, she thought, you really don't know how ready I have to be for you, do you? You really don't know how I walk, turn, uncurl, or even touch my own thigh, like I'm doing now, just for you.

But she only really called to him once when she saw him put away his studies to write, haltingly at first, in a journal.

"Are you saying that you wish for ten or maybe a hundred more naked females at your beck and call?" she asked.

"No," he said, looking into the thin, straight branches over his head. "I'm writing about the swallows, the ones that were over the tent this morning. And about the kingfisher I think I saw in that cove yesterday."

Late in the day, when the tops of the trees across the lake were fired by sunlight, Colin crawled out onto the rock next to Nicki's with the binoculars in his hands. Lying on his stomach and wiping his sweaty fingers on his shorts, he searched the opposite shoreline for what he wanted to see. Feeding heron. Beaver. The trailing ripples of leaping bass. As she lay upon the worn and pitted stone, the breeze passing between her knees while she watched him, Nicki fingered a mussel shell that she had found wedged between two of the rocks. Its gray edges were chipped and ragged. Its surfaces were bleached and crusty to the touch. But it's so beautiful in my head, she thought, like Colin's so beautiful in my head. With his smile. With his legs stretched out behind him on that rock. And his hands, he never stops his hands in my mind, not ever.

As Colin pointed a finger at a sighted heron, Nicki climbed off the rock to cover herself and to pull her thick hair away from her sunburned face. I'll have to bring it up again, she told herself, or I won't be able to stand it anymore. They're staying with me, getting taller and darker in the shadows, and I'm starting to hate them—the boys, the men in bright sweaters and coats that he only looks at once. I'm learning to hate every one of them.

Colin took a bath just as the sun set. Nicki watched him shampoo as she built a small fire for dinner. He was happy rinsing himself and eyeing a pair of loons that were beginning to feed a few hundred yards to the north. He growled, filling the quiet as he bent over to shake the clear water from his hair. She loved him, envied him as he stood calmly naked in the cold, caressing ripples of the lake. His stomach was flat and hard. His thighs were longer, sturdier than her own. He moved smoothly, and Nicki couldn't find any distraction or worry in the way he cleansed his body. But it has to be there, she told herself. He has to feel like the water is the touch of some man's cool fingers on his knees.

"Hey you," he called to her, his shoulders glistening in the falling light. "You with the can opener and the burn. I could use a little help here. How would you like to dry my back?"

She rubbed his dark skin until he turned toward her and caught her hands up in the heavy blue towel, drawing them to his chest. He kissed her, with damp lips, on the forehead.

"You're awfully quiet," he said. "In fact, you're too quiet. Will you look up here and tell me what's wrong?" But Nicki said nothing as she turned back to tend her fire. She started to walk away, her shoulders in a tight shrug. "I know," he said, his soft voice blending behind her with the breeze. "I guess I didn't really have to ask you. It's the same. I know it is. You want me to make love to you. Don't you?"

She felt him try to prove everything to her. The stroke of a hand here, here. The moist brush of lips there, there, again. She felt him try to take hold of her desire and his love and caress them into a tenderness that would stay with them beyond the comfort of the goose down and smooth, slippery nylon they rolled upon. So as she lay upon him, their stomachs slick and joined with perspiration, she wiped his first tears away with her fingers.

"It's okay, it's okay, it's okay," she whispered. But she knew it wasn't. He talked like that, Colin was the one who spoke like that to keep the memories in his mind, to keep their legs and their chests from filling the tent and crowding his life. She couldn't talk them away. She could only soothe him because she couldn't see his face in the blackened tent and he was crying, as always, without a sound. "I love you, Colin," she said as she rolled off him so that she could encircle him, keep him warm, with her bare arms and legs. She flinched a little when he placed a hand on her belly and said nothing. She was afraid he was saying to himself like he had said to her that when he had sons—and he would have them—he would never name one after himself.

She thought he was asleep when she felt him turn away from her, huddled in his sleeping bag, breathing evenly, more slowly. She stroked his uncurled fingers for an hour, two hours, as she listened to the owls move deeper into the woods and watched the rising moonlight filter through the blue fibers of the tent and streak his hair. But finally she rose and put on the clothes she could find—her jeans, her boots and socks—and, wrapping her shoulders in a towel, crawled out of the tent and into the dark.

The moving light of the water drew her toward the rocks. They were broad and falsely smooth beneath the moon. Sitting on the largest one with her long hair swinging in her eyes, Nicki shivered in the emptiness that had settled in with the night. She pressed her legs and her hands against the stone.

It was still warm from the sun. She could smell the hot, dry dust of its crumbling. Catching her boot heels in two rain-worn crevices along the rock's side, she leaned forward and looked and spread herself so far across the water that she almost didn't hear him. But he stepped on a twig, snapping his presence across the distance between them. His jeans hung loosely around his bare, narrow hips. His face was cut across with shadows. Climbing the rock and standing behind her, he filled one of his tired hands with her hair.

"Nicki," he said. "You know I want. . . ."

"Yes," she said. "I know."

Together, they stayed on the edge of the shore listening for any sound in the night that would take them further away than the echoes of the owls at their backs. They stayed there—hand to hand, shoulder to shoulder—until the gray light of morning unveiled the water to the first dives of the kingfishers.

Where Men Go to Cry

"He had the kind of beauty which defends itself from any caress."
—Virginia Woolf, *The Waves*

It was the fatigue that introduced them. On the night Linnea took him home, Paul arranged his drawing board in his customary spot near the back wall. He preferred to let the models stride in, pose, and choose his profiles for him. This time, Linnea set up beside him, just to his right. The model was a young woman, a lean girl that Paul thought he recognized from the local bookstore. He was not surprised when she stepped onto the dais—naked and slim—facing away from him, her long spine curving toward Linnea. Linnea, of course, said nothing. She merely began to sketch—even while the instructor completed his opening remarks—her small hand circling swiftly above the paper before it bore down.

Paul had only managed to fling a few light lines onto his page before Linnea slumped, badly. He had been taking his time with the form of the model's buttocks because he wanted to be sure of what he saw there. When Linnea slumped, her round chin sagging onto the ribbed collar of her sweater, he took his time with that image also. He didn't want to get involved. But when Linnea—her eyes trained on the drawing before her—reached for her cheek with a wavering, unguided hand, he leaned politely toward her.

"Are you all right?" he asked, looking past her at the red-haired woman at the next table, not wanting to be rude.

Linnea nodded rather firmly, her eyes closed, her hand still grasping for her face as if it were after something sinking in water. "I am fine, thank you. Just weak." He noted that her voice was strung hard, without accent. "Are *you* all right?"

Paul was immediately embarrassed. Linnea was looking right at him, directly into his chest, her unsteadiness apparently cleared away by the force of her words. He noticed, in his discomfort, that though she was not a thin woman, her black sweater engulfed her in a way that made her appear breastless, almost mannish.

"I suppose," he said.

"Good," she answered. "You can help me carry my things. I need to get home."

He was glad, at least, that she allowed him the one thing he took pride in—his efficiency. He placed her charcoal in its box, strapped her shadowy sketch into her firm portfolio, all while she sat on a stool coolly mesmerized by the model's still, white flesh. When he had gathered Linnea's belongings with his, they left the studio one after another, Paul opening the door to the hallway and nodding to the instructor while Linnea slipped out. He was relieved that the other students took little notice of their departure, the soft rasp of charcoal and expressive breathing remaining constant as he turned to leave. Life drawing for him, after all, was a brief hobby, something to do while he waited to leave the country. And Linnea, well, she was obviously talented enough to serve her own whims. Everyone in the class, including the instructor, had to know that. It was Paul's only hope, as he shut the paint-spattered door behind them, that his fellow students didn't also know that he had worked hard to manage this exit; that he, at all costs, had not wanted to leave the light of the studio as if he were just churning flotsam in the wake of this woman Linnea.

The bay breeze was fresh but cool, and Paul felt the skin of his legs crawl as he followed Linnea down the few brick steps that led to the street. Rain was a possibility. The stretches of horizon that he could see between the waterfront warehouses were mottled with the fringe of a cloud bank. After he helped Linnea, he told himself, he would have to hurry home before the car was bathed in a heavy, salt-bearing wind.

"I live on Spring Street, exactly fourteen hundred steps away," she said as they reached the herring-bone sidewalk. "I hope you don't mind."

"Not at all," he said, surprised that there was no shiver in her voice. "Not if you will count."

Silence. The shuffle of her flat, cotton slippers on the brick. Paul blushed under his pressed shirt collar. He had wanted to be funny, not biting, not the final word. But this woman had her ideas, and she was weak, perhaps actually ill. He nodded to himself, recognizing the duties of good manners and kindness, and began to follow her whispering steps into the night, hoping at each moment to catch up and move up beside her.

The neighborhood they climbed into was old, only barely rubbed by the distant sounds of the expressway. The houses were hillside remnants, the squarebuilt homes of the merchants who sailed in and out of Portland a hundred years before. Paul's mother had often driven him into that very part of town because, she said, one should develop a clear eye for design. He had always liked his tours. Even now, as they passed a grand clapboard façade, he thought he could smell fresh-cut flowers—the sort his mother adored—though he had to struggle for clarity. The vapors of paint and turpentine rose strongly from Linnea.

"It's my parent's house, this gray one," she said, leading him onto a small varnished porch. "They stay up north now, though. Permanently."

"Nice," he said, examining a carefully restored portico. "Historic."

"Yes." She sounded mildly exasperated, irritable. "You'll have to take my things in, you know. My studio's upstairs."

Once inside, Linnea gamely negotiated the narrow spiral staircase that led from the foyer to the open second floor. Paul could tell that it was a struggle because, even from behind, the deep round intake of her breath was audible. He also noticed what he hadn't seen before—the drag and lean of a slight limp, a crookedness now quite visible in her step.

The studio was still dark when he reached the top of the staircase. Moving toward a black shape that he took to be a table, Paul shifted Linnea's portfolio from under his arm and prepared to lay it down. From somewhere to his left he could hear the suck of breathing.

"No, not there," she told him. "Here. With me."

"Is it clear?" he asked. "The path, I mean. I don't want to ruin anything."

"Just follow my voice," she said.

She turned on a lamp when he was perhaps two steps away, his free hand outstretched, his lips tight with concentration. For a long moment the vaguely lit studio wavered huge in Paul's eyes: four rooms stripped of everything usual except their wallpaper; mantels and windowsills lined with brushes and erasers; doorless closets stacked with canvases. In one corner there was a green easy chair, a coffee-maker, an uneven stack of magazines and Boston newspapers. A squat radio was on a nearby table. The back wall was covered with sketches of twirling, shifting bodies. Easel after easel, frame upon frame, the rooms gave themselves to the craft at hand.

Paul found himself trying not to stare.

"Yes, it's damn large," Linnea said, her fingers still on the lamp that he could now see was polished brass. "I'm spoiled. My parents, as I said, have moved."

"It's a tremendous opportunity," he said, leaning her portfolio against the bannister, afraid to step away from the staircase until she did.

"I'd say so."

She did not invite him to sit down, to relax, or even help her move some of her larger paintings. Instead, she seemed intent only on looking at him. Without attempting to be polite, she fixed her eyes on him and watched, her fingers kneading the hem of her sweater as she shifted her chin. Paul glanced back at her for the shortest space of time, feeling imposed upon, but the depth of her pupils was too much. Eventually, he found himself staring patiently into the cup of his clasped hands, wondering why she was testing him.

"Shitty light in here, Paul. Would you hit the switches by the mantel over there? All of them."

He took his time. He wanted to be careful. Then, with two movements of his thumb, the room they were standing in, the southeastern one, was fully lit, unshadowed. Paul immediately understood that he was in the naked objectivity of a gallery.

"I thought so," Linnea said from behind him where she was still guarded by the lamp.

"What? What did I do?"

"Brown hair. Brown eyes. Fine buttocks. It's been hard to

tell up to now, but I was right. About 185 centimeters. A small Praxiteles Hermes."

Paul smiled, wanting to be ironic. "I measure up?"

"You are a beautiful specimen," she said, rubbing her eyes with hands that now looked plump enough to be nearly flaccid. "That much is clear. If I weren't so tired, I might ask you to take your shirt off although I know, already, what your back has to look like. They must have tried to get you to model down there."

Paul ran his fingers through his hair. "Yes," he said. "They tried."

"But you said no, didn't you." Linnea stepped toward him, her palms out flat, surveying the air before her. "You told them no because I know you, Paul," she said, looking squarely at him, "and I know that you wouldn't show your balls to anyone."

It took a moment. Then Paul felt his stomach tighten beneath his ribs. "I'd better go,," he said, carefully. "I hope you're not ill."

"Don't be a jerk," she said. "I'm not insulting you. I'm only telling the truth. The studio went after you because they have wonderful taste down there and they couldn't resist. You didn't go for it." She stopped with her fingers in a grip which punched out at the level of his waist. "Because you're so private. That much is easy to tell."

"I had my reasons."

"As you always do, I'm sure. Come here, then, and I'll show you something. Get this friendship started. So that you'll stop looking like some whore has asked you to drop your pants."

Paul followed her into the next room, a tiny solarium that contained only one easel and a chair. The canvas on the easel was covered with a dark blue cloth. He stopped just inside the doorway, letting Linnea fill the room with her weight. As he arranged a series of deep breaths, one after another, he realized that he was sweating.

"Just so you'll know that I'm not after your ass," she said, lifting the cloth from the top of the easel, "let me show you what I've already got. It's not perfect, but it is determined. And, thank God, it is not skittishly private."

Paul expected nudity. What he saw instead was motion, concentration, vigor—all clothed in the garish design of sport. A baseball player, a well-muscled man twisting his way through the batter's box wearing a uniform that seemed as pure and personal as skin.

"Who is he?" Paul was caught off guard. A sports hero? An idol? He had imagined something a little more obscure. More artistic, maybe.

"An infielder, an outfielder. It can't matter to you," she said, looking unabashedly at her own work. "I am thirty-five years old, I am dying. This man is my purity. I could break it down for you, but I won't." She turned toward him and took him in by parts—his head and shoulders, his torso, his crotch. "I can't show you what you can't know," she said.

"You are a very fine artist," he said.

Linnea laughed. "I will trust your judgment, of course."

Paul watched her walk to a bank of small windows that overlooked the edge of the bay. The badly-installed track lighting cut across her face and broke harshly over her hair which he could see was quite dull at the roots. Despite the fact that this woman was obviously baiting him, her face began to etch itself in his mind. Thin, straggling eyebrows. A complexion the uneven color and texture of winter sand. She was, he knew now, quite ugly. But as the narrowness of her shoulders trembled into the ill breadth of her hips, Paul felt his manners give way to interest, to what he might have initially and unkindly called pity. Faced with the wrenching grimace of a nameless ballplayer, what would it be like to touch this woman, he wondered. What would it feel like to feel Linnea?

He came to see her the next day, bringing flowers and two newspapers. "I wasn't sure you'd be able to get out," he said as she answered the door. "I don't have your phone number."

"You are too polite, Paul," she said, taking the bouquet of freesia and laying it in a chair before she frowned at him. "I should have expected as much. There is some coffee ready upstairs."

He followed her to the studio after he put the flowers in a vase he found in the kitchen. Linnea had left them behind.

It was clear that she was intent on being gruff or at least blunt with him. The edge that had just shown itself the night before was now clean and unhidden. But he would endure it. She had, after all, issued a challenge of some sort. And God knows, he had few other distractions. How could it hurt?, he asked himself. What could it bother?

In the unbroken daylight of the studio, Linnea looked close to wretched. Her straight, homecut hair was drawn against its will into a thin and uneven ponytail. The brightly patterned housecoat that was snapped tight around her throat did nothing but accentuate the pallor of her face and the disconcerting weakness of her small chin. Looking at her crumpled in her easy chair, Paul realized that it was only the eyes, the still-burning eyes, that held her face together.

"I'm not good today," she said, rubbing her broad, blotched forehead. "I have nothing to say."

"Boston won last night." Paul cleared his throat with his hand over his mouth. He'd worked hard, scanning the morning papers, for that fact. "That's really my only message. I was just wondering . . . ."

"The score was 4-2. Lee gave up six hits. Rice homered. Hobson, thank God, picked up an RBI. The team is now 5½ games out with a current batting average of, let me think. .262."

"I'm sorry."

"For what? For bothering me? Forget it. You can always try to be nice to me," she said, looking at him with two fists curled in her lap. "I just may not like it. As I said, I am dying."

"I'm . . . ."

"Don't you dare apologize for that either." She was shouting now, her voice rising with a heave of her well-covered chest. Somewhere in his head, Paul heard the thud of her own hands against her body. "Just tell me what you want, you fucking beautiful thing. Do you want to be painted? Is that it?"

Paul turned and began to walk, his shoulders slightly hunched. She was exploding, her mouth twisting, her cheeks shaking with sobs. He had not meant to cause that or see it or even ever hear about it. He had just wanted to be nice, to do something that involved a little good spirit before he left to begin his fieldwork.

Did she have the right to ask him those things? He supposed so. From her perspective he must appear to be the worst. An opportunist, a vulture, a camera's eye.

Behind him Linnea blew her nose, signalling to him, he thought, her intention to continue their what? . . . their conversation? Threading his way through the clutter of the studio, Paul decided he would wait for her in the solarium. In there, at least, everything but the light was sparse and controlled.

"Okay," she said from the doorway, her voice softened by swallowed tears. "Why are you here? If you don't want to have that fine butt painted?"

Paul watched the ferry to Nova Scotia glide through Casco Bay. Its motion, even as it edged past the abandoned oil docks, was remarkably predictable. "To be honest, I'm leaving the country in just over a month to finish school, graduate school. I can't answer your question really. I'm at loose ends."

He heard Linea move behind him, smelled the deep, free smells of her body. It occurred to him that she might be arranging herself for him. "Sit down," she said, somehow having the words warm the back of his neck. "In the chair. I've got some coffee for the two of us."

It was Linnea who suggested that they take things one at a time. "I don't see my old friends anymore, not even the artists. I'm very conscious of having driven them away." She sat on the stained wooden floor of the solarium, a coffee cup balanced on her knee. "But you're untested. We can try to work something out."

"I'll be leaving in five weeks or so. I don't think I'm dangerous." He wanted to stretch out in the chair, but its straight back only allowed for one posture—upright, face forward. "I will not be an imposition though. Only if you need something."

"I need someone to watch me, that's all. My work is changing very quickly. I'd like a measure for that." She nodded toward the covered easel. "Where are you going, anyway?"

"Upper Volta. In Africa."

She laughed, her small teeth spreading above her tongue. For a second, the shape of her face changed completely. "I should have known, I should have known," she said.

"Why?"

"Because there's no hint of it anywhere. Your person is discreet."

"It's true." He smiled back. "I don't own a single dashiki."

"You know what I mean though, Paul," she said, lowering her voice. "You are hiding. You try to tell almost nothing."

So he told her that he was preparing to finish his PhD. That he would be a half day's drive from Ouagadougou studying a small village of Bobo tribesmen for a year, maybe two. Afterwards, there would be the dissertation, long months in the library at Berkeley, the degree, a teaching job somewhere in the East. He told her he knew that his plans were thin, vastly general, but if he'd learned one thing from his professors, he said, it was this: you had to be patient. Even in the hot, dry, sub-Saharan winds, you had to be patient.

"I'm packed and ready, I guess," he concluded. "As ready as I'll ever be."

Linnea shook her head. "There is a lot you're not admitting to Paul. I can see it. It's all marked out there in your hands. And your jawline." She pointed at him. "You're older, better forged, than you make out to be. Come on. What about the friends, the parents, the bits and pieces of old lovers?"

He did not like her sudden animation. He had hoped that she, at least, would take only what her eye would give her. Shifting his weight in the chair he watched her push her awkward hips against the door jamb so that she could face him, her eyes resting uneasily beneath the edge of her stringy bangs. "There isn't much to tell, really," he said. "My parents and my brother live an hour away. I've spent the last three years of my life in classrooms. Before that I traveled a little."

Paul sighed somewhere deep in his throat. He was sinking; he could feel it. A brief passage from Tchaikovski's 6th slipped into his mind and echoed. Her passage, someone else's march. God, even the most veiled references to his past were capable of pulling him back and down. He told himself that he should know that by now.

"No, no," Linnea said. "I want you to try that again. Or better yet, let me try it." Paul could see that her right hand was uncommonly alive as it stroked the worn grain of the floorboards before her. Her fingertips slid as if driven by static. "I am tired of wasting time," she said. "I see things, things that you just barely feel."

Paul put his hands in his pockets. She was pushing him again.

"I don't care about Berkeley," she said. "You've left a woman somewhere. You've perhaps had men or wanted men—you're lovely enough for that—but recently it's been this woman. She's blond, probably in school, and very tall, taller than I am. But her face is not important. It's what you carry with you in the dark that wants to kill you. This woman—she's plaintive, she loves you, she has a softness to her skin that you want, above everything, to forget. You've scared yourself because you've noticed that her small, even breasts have nipples the color of your lips and you're fascinated. Her shoulders are the width of your hips, her wet hair smells faintly like your mother's, her voice has a tone that you've never been able to freeze or break apart. You've noticed all this. You hate it. It's eating you alive."

"You flatter yourself," Paul said, forcing himself to look out to sea.

"I'm not finished yet," Linnea said, both hands working the floor. "The foremost fact is that you've left her. Cleared out. Neat and tidy. Now you're burying her—in sub-Saharan sand, I'd guess. And you know why?"

Paul felt his shell of polite interest shift a bit. Strangely, there was no note of pride in Linnea's declaration. He thought back. No, she'd never done more than narrate. He wondered. Was she baiting him again?

"You do know," she continued. "So do I. You did it because you were afraid you couldn't feel anything. Not that right thing, anyway. You made love to her a hundred times maybe—probably to symphonies, sounds that you chose—but something, something you expected didn't happen."

Paul laughed over the small catch in his throat. "You tell quite a story."

"I'm not wrong about this, Paul. You carry yourself like a ramrod, imperturbable or something. But it's all a defense. Something's broken."

"Her name is Susan," he said. "She is not blond."

"She loves you though, doesn't she?" Linnea was flickering behind her bangs again.

"She's younger."

"I don't mean to pry. I just don't have time. And I have to, have to read the faces I've got."

"Don't worry," Paul said, standing and looking out over the water again. "You only got it half right. It's been worked out."

"You don't see her. Or anybody."

Linnea's voice, he thought, was very cold music. Her age, he supposed.

"I'm going to Africa."

If he had had his way, everything would have ended there at noon in a sunlit pool of understanding. But it did not. Now, Linnea could not let him go. He was sure he recognized the signs: a woman temporarily bound by silence, temporarily romanced by tenderness. He heard her push herself up the cream-colored wall with her feet. When she was standing, he realized he was afraid she would move toward him to offer more coffee, to trap him.

"I should be on my way," he said.

The intake of her breath was audible, but it was not followed by admonishment or anger or the scurry of embarrassment. Instead, the piercing clarity of her words dove through him and left him hollow. "I only want to know," she said, "what it's like to be beautiful. Look at me, Paul. You'll know why."

He couldn't gather himself soon enough to help her to the chair. She limped there by herself—broken, red, and furious at her weakness. There were tears in her narrowed eyes and a crippled fury in her shoulders which seemed to shiver into a control of its own. Paul couldn't quite say that she was crying, but she was, it was obvious to him, in some sort of deep, unmet pain.

"Why else do you think I'm so foolish?" she asked. "Look at him, look at *him*," she said throwing her voice at the covered canvas of the baseball player. "I've painted him over and over again. I've met him, talked to him, leaned on the edge of my ballpark seat when he's on the field. And what is he? A ballplayer. A man. An exquisitely proportioned machine of bone and muscle." Paul felt the arc of the painting's hidden motion cut through cloth and air. Its finely rendered twist made its way into Linnea's voice. "And for some god-damned reason I'm cursed with him. I want to know him, I want to know that lovely capturing urge before it's over." She stopped then, her hair loose from her ponytail, dangling about her face and neck like a worn fringe. Paul did not move. He found himself seeing, acquiring, overcome with the setting composition of a picture. One of Linnea's hands fell into her lap like a claw. The other dropped flat, its flutter deadened. An open palm, an offering, a half prayer.

Over the course of the month before he left for Africa, Linnea explained her illness to Paul. She was careful in her divulgence, always speaking to him as if she was teaching him something, impressing him with cold factual details that he ought to remember. When the sclerosis in her left hand worsened, she opened her books of Renaissance reproductions and showed him—as only she could—the changes in her flesh and structure.

"It's here and here, now," she would say, pressing the gloss of a DaVinci and then his own waiting hand with a finger. "It will only get worse, but not steadily. Every day is different. And I know enough not to grieve over surprises."

She was resolutely cheerful even though they both knew it was a game. She would return from her occasional visits to the clinic smiling stiffly, her sketch pad covered with cross-hatched drawings of Paul's face, Paul's arms. On her worst days, when she could barely speak and her face hung like lifeless parchment, she would share their rare laughter by tapping her knuckles or a loosely-swung elbow on her thigh. It was important, she said, for her to keep moving. She had things to accomplish.

But Paul did not have the same driven, finite ambitions. Even before Linnea told him in her most cutting manner that he was drifting, he knew it. The nights of anxious dreams that had ranged his mind in the spring—singing to him in pidgin French, pinning him in blinding, unbroken sunlight—gave way to tiny, fragmented visions and sleeplessness. Except in early morning, when he was still in bed and the ocean was the only boundary he could imagine, it was difficult to conjure up Africa.

He could hardly believe he was going. The only reality he felt sure of was an awkward consciousness of his body. What he carried from day to day were his tendons, his graceful bones, whatever Linnea seemed to have left with him the day before. And being faced with his own nakedness—in the shower, beneath the looseness of his summer clothing—shocked him, froze him up. It took Linnea to help him stay in motion.

"I would like to finish one series before you leave," she told him. It was one of her good days. She was wearing a sleeveless red blouse with a daisy dangling in a buttonhole. "More of the baseball stuff. I thought I could do it with your help."

Paul looked at her swaying next to an easel, honest and childlike, her hair pushed back by a blue stretch band. "Baseball? Now?" Her preoccupations still surprised him.

She laughed. "Of course. Their motion is the hardest to follow, Paul. Hardest to reduce. Whatever those men do, they do fast. And alone."

But why not dancers, he wanted to ask. Or just models? Still he didn't question her; he couldn't. He was afraid of what would happen if Linnea ever really thought her fragility was foolish.

"I don't know if I can help," he said. "I don't have many skills like that."

"Just hold a pallet for me." Linnea stomped her foot, perhaps as a joke. "Hold things for me. You always expect so many demands."

It was then that they began to touch each other, tenderly and without secret. Linnea kept it in the air, calling him handsome to his face, pretending to pinch at his skin in rushes of energy. But Paul knew it to be someting different, something that he considered too daring and ragged for the both of them. Though he did nothing to change it. Their fingers locked and unlocked as he passed paint and brushes, and he took this home with him to his small, spartan bedroom where it began to curl into his sleep. Time is my arbiter, he thought when he was most anxious. Time will separate us and somehow, as it always does, remake the pain.

Paul then imagined a satisfactory separation into being. He composed what he considered to be a workable plan while he ate his breakfast of toast and poached egg during the habitual time he gave to himself before he visited Linnea. He would spend a few days with his parents; Susan would come into his life for a weekend, a last passage of native joy. Linnea would be his first and most private farewell, but he would have done with it. Dinner, a small, well-chosen gift and perhaps, well, a brief engulfing physical contact that would swallow him until he actually left for Paris en route to Dakar and Ouagadougou. He would allow for that possibility and prepare, immediately, to move beyond it. As he drank his morning coffee, looking from his apartment toward the wharves, he was pleased with his own frank thoughts. He could think of being with Linnea—sleeping with her—and it didn't paralyze him. He would, after all, see her in a few months. Nothing would be begun or finished with his departure. As she had told him, her disease was a slow, mysterious, inaccurate one. She could and would, she hoped, live for years.

But Linnea cut him off, beat him to the final mark. When he arrived one morning with a can of linseed oil, some milk and fresh fruit, she answered the door hurriedly, with a sheen of sweat above her lip. "I'm on the phone to Boston," she said. "They want me there tomorrow to start on Hobson, lovely Hobson, and Rice." She went into the kitchen, back to the phone. Vaguely, Paul realized that she was hardly dressed. Her thick, pale legs were bare; her dressing gown was open past her breasts. As she spoke, loudly and surely into the phone, Paul sat at the foot of the polished staircase, the bag of oil and groceries pressed close to his ribs.

"The front office has seen some of my work," she said, coming into the foyer with her robe pulled tight around her swollen figure. "They want some paintings, at least two. I can hardly turn them down."

"They will be wonderful," he said. "I'm sure."

"The best I can do. Given the time."

"Do you think you will get it this time, this energy or beauty that you want?" He set the groceries on the floor, hoping their rattle would half cover the wry thickness of his question.

Linnea stopped, her mouth an unconscious dent, before she walked past him toward her bedroom. "This reminds me of the time I left Claude," she said. "In New York or Paris, I can't remember. It was over before the door shut."

"You're leaving tomorrow?"

"For quite awhile, I'm afraid. I'm sorry," she said, turning the corner to her room. Paul could barely hear her. "I didn't plan it this way."

But she had planned it. He knew that. Linnea was so desperate about her time—her dwindling time, she called it—that she had not dropped a single moment into the well of open possibility since he had met her. Boston and her ballplayer must have been in the works for weeks; the unsteadiness of her illness allowed for no less. Paul was momentarily furious. How dare she refuse to face him before he left the continent and the only risk he had taken since he put Susan back from his body and his mind. She knew it was a risk, his being with her and squeezing himself under the lens of her peculiarly magnified world. She knew he trusted her. And she had turned away.

"Life is often like that," he said, raising his voice so that it might follow her into the closet. "It turns swiftly. Susan and I lost each other that way."

"Martìn," she shouted back. "Martìn . . . I told you about him . . . he is the one I clung to. I was young. And he was so handsome."

When she emerged some minutes later, Paul was pacing, circling the area near her old stereo. A Bach recording was on the turntable, but he had not yet placed the needle in its groove. He was wondering if he should go upstairs or just leave. After all, he and Linnea had never listened to music together.

"A good idea," she said, pausing several feet away from him. "I'll get some wine. We should probably celebrate."

He watched her enter the kitchen. A woman who was, he realized, a sack of shuffled desires and disappointments. He did not miss the fact that she was dressed just as she had been the night he met her. Dark pants, the black misshapen sweater, her hair free and clean around her face. Linnea did not err. Though the female in her might seem buried in her determination, she did not make mistakes.

Then it would just be over. She could not blame him. He

had come and gone from her life like a bout of bad weather. Or a sickness. Yes, that was it. Illness bred illness, and he had been like a functional fever. Linnea, working from her stubborn heart, had conquered him in order to cure herself.

He had been used. Pressing a button and taking in the swift ascension of Bach's fugue, Paul allowed himself to think of Susan, to look somewhere in himself for the symptoms of time-killing desire. The scent of her light skin was like . . . was like . . . .

But again, Linnea could not let him go. At least he perceived her distant graciousness that way. "I think we should toast ourselves upstairs," she said, moving quietly past him. "When the music is over, of course."

He found her slouched in her green armchair, an uncorked bottle of chardonnay by her feet. He thought he could smell the wine: a new, heavy perfume. Linnea seemed distracted, the white moon of her chin resting on her knuckles. But she stood when Paul cleared the top of the staircase. "Cheers," she said. "I think we should forgive each other."

"For what?" he asked, impatiently surveying the studio. "Our lack of manners?"

"No, our wish to get out. Leave." She dropped back into her chair, gracelessly. "You know what I mean."

"No, I don't. I wanted to do this without . . . I wanted to do it right."

"You want to do everything right."

Paul looked over her worktables, her scattered sketches and pallets. It was all there—shape, blending, a variety of flesh tones. "I wanted to give you something," he said.

"What?" she said, a fresh edge in her voice. "You never made love to me. You never even told me what it was like with Susan. I don't see that you've given me anything that's worth a fuck."

"That's all you wanted, then." He spoke through his set teeth, anger moving to trembling in his knees.

"No, I think that's all you wanted. An ugly woman, some adoration. A pitiful piece of leave-taking ass." Linea rocked herself with rage, though her chair was anchored and ungiving. The wine bottle rattled at her heels.

"You're bitter," he said.

"No, you are," she shouted, hammering the air with a whole arm. "You god damn fucking are."

Paul left her, the broken tattoo of her pounding feet following him down the stairs and through the bare foyer. She wasn't helpless, he told himself. She never had been. A woman like that would eat him alive.

He only made it to Ouagadougou about once a month. The American attaché and his wife were always encouraging him to visit, to give himself time to adjust to the broad, unbroken patterns of the village. But Paul was hard on himself; he insisted on making it all work, allowing himself time off only when he needed supplies—batteries, film, new cassettes. He wasn't worried about burnout. Where could he go, where would he want to go if he failed?

At the end of the rainy season, he gave himself a brief vacation, a trip east to the sacred crocodile lake at Sabou. On his way back, he stopped in Ouagadougou for a complete French meal at the attaché's expense and a mail check.

In his fan-cooled hotel room, Paul opened a bulky packet from his mother. Inside, he found a heavy cotton shirt, two English novels, and an envelope of newspaper clippings. His mother also included a lengthy letter spiced with dry, crisp wit and pertinent news from home. She answered his various questions and praised him for his frequent and detailed correspondence. It remains so fascinating, even on the page, she wrote. Your tales from Africa have you sounding so strong and well.

Paul read her letter twice before he folded it beneath the fly-leaf of one of the novels. He wondered if he would ever tell her how bad it was.

The envelope of clippings contained two surprises. The first was a brief letter from Susan saying that she might or might not fly into Dakar for a Christmas visit. The stationary was cool and very smooth in his hand. Reading her rounded handwriting, Paul felt his heart beat with the thud of the Belgian-made window fan. He needed her to visit. Weeks ago he had realized, rather crudely, what it meant to need a woman. The warm native malt, the exquisitely barren landscape, the bound and shifting sun were never enough. The scents and sighs of the Bobo women were only cruel flavoring. He was not quite in love with Susan, but he had told her that. She hadn't seemed to mind. I'm trying, her letter said, to work something out.

The last surprise was a trio of postcards addressed to him in care of his parents. They all bore Portland postmarks. Their messages were brief. *I'm sorry. I'm sorry. Thank you.* Paul flipped them over, spreading them out on the poorly-dyed bedspread. DaVinci. Michelangelo. DaVinci.

Linnea. She had done it to him. Caught him in the middle. He tried to remember if he had thought of her since the flight from Paris to Dakar when he dreamed that he slept with her, dreamed that he made love to her as her skin moved like dough. In that turbulent sleep, she had pulled him into her as if his thrusts, his flesh, his desires were never-ending. She had read his face with her fingers while they moved together. No, no, he convinced himself that he had not thought of her. But she had gotten to him in any case. *I'm sorry.* She must be dying. *Thank you.*

He would call her. The cards were, according to their dates, more than three weeks old. But where would she be? The hospital? With her parents? Under the care of a twenty-four hour nurse who, Linnea used to say, would surely be cursedly color blind? Paul left the hotel with his wallet, following the vague directions of the drowsy concierge. The Intertel booth was only a few blocks away.

What would he say to her? Paul remembered the way she had named the sunlight as it changed through the arc of a day, moving from the broad sea gray of early morning to the hot, unforgiving shafts of noon. Notice the difference when you're away, Paul, she had said. The dawn will be so different when you're in Africa. The dusk will be so harsh.

He stopped on a broken street corner, already sweating. A young native boy tried desperately to sell him a newspaper, then some fruit. What would he say to her? A woman who couldn't speak, who might be paralyzed or even—he looked at the sky—dead. Here I am, Linnea. Not so far away. Here I am. In a country where even the mighty Mossi emperor still rules cross-legged in the dust.

Nongqause

Nongqause is a high priestess. Or so she enjoys telling me. I have a certain power, she says, sitting on her small Persian rug, handing me a cup of coffee. I can tell you things, Kirby. Things you need to know.

I don't always laugh at this because I like to think that Nongqause, or Neilanne as she is known to most people, is the most actively mysterious person in my life. She has decided today, for instance, to let her hair grow out this winter, and I can be sure that by Christmas her black hair will be long, long, practically to her shoulder blades. I am not really sure how she will do this, but I know it will happen. Because I believe there is something special there. Neilanne is ripe and changing, and she always has been. Which is why I find time to visit her.

"Take men," she says on this clear afternoon. "They are a prize if they find the way."

"Oh yes," I say laughing. "But mostly they are *in* the way."

Nongqause frowns at me, her index finger tapping the stack of enameled tarot cards she keeps near the hearth. "Kirby, you are edging up to bitterness. You're not listening."

I nod, trying to regain a certain kind of composure. Nongqause and I have walked this path many times. She never seems to tire of it even though she knows how I feel, what I've done about Larry. "I'm sorry," I say. "I just think I know what you're leading up to."

"Don't think. Listen," she says. "That's my first rule."

So I listen to her start her engines. She has noticed a few things about the men next door, the men she shares this peeling, rambling farmhouse with. She lists some facts she thinks I ought to be aware of.

"They are all single over there," she says, leaning in the

direction of the east wing. "Or close enough. Most of them work. Every one has a car." She spreads her hands over her Indian block-print skirt. "They are my chance."

"What?" I tell myself I shouldn't be afraid of this.

"Big chance."

I start to protest or make some kind of stink without spilling my coffee, but Nongqause waves to me to be quiet, pointing at the books that are piled behind the tarot cards, near a neat stack of kindling. "I've been reading like you said. Cassandra may have been a pain, but she was right on the money."

"The Trojans won," I say, shaking my head, thinking that Marie was right. I have created a monster.

"There are five of them over there," she says. "Can't miss."

Neilanne, you see, has moved out to the farm to prepare herself for a new turn in life, another crack at the community college. She's left a lot of things behind—an almost ex-husband, a job leasing apartments for a local management corporation. All with my blessing. She's also left her last name, her TV, and her touch-tone phone back in town where she says they truly belong, so for the last six months she has been hard to get in touch with. For the most part, I've considered this natural. A little dramatic, but natural.

"They've been asking about your car," she continues.

"The Chevrolet? What's there to ask," I say. "It's paid for."

"Jim was directly curious. I saw him this afternoon."

I slap my knee. Jim, as Neilanne in her more familiar moments has already told me, is a twenty-three year old law student. Young enough to be my littlest brother, young enough to be a bad, bad temptation.

"He drives a brand new Honda," I remind her. "There's no turning back from a man like that."

Nongqause, with her determined face and quiet hands, is exasperated with me. "You might try to be serious about this," she says, gracefully aligning her vertebra until she is regal as a cobra. And as cold. "I have thought it out. It will be different this time. I will not beg, I will be. I believed you understood."

My cheeks flush a little, even in the draftiness of the old living room. I still do this to Neilanne; I underestimate her. I did it to Larry, and it cost me, but I guess I haven't learned.

Neilanne *has* worked hard. She has lost weight, given up makeup, made herself read well into the night. She has also, almost as a joke, stopped wearing bras in favor of those tight t-shirts that show off her breasts. Not that she burned her underwires or anything. No, her symbols are more personal than that. But she has made some adjustments. Often we laugh about this—like when we plan for the nude sunbathing we want to do next summer—but the laughter is the froth. In our minds, Neilanne has to be Nongqause or Cassandra or Judith, conqueror of Holofernes. At least for a while.

"I do understand," I say, looking into her black water eyes. "I'm sorry."

"This is not about sex," she says, relaxing a little. "Remember. I've made a big decision about that. Sex is not in there, not up front." She taps the cards again, and I know she's reminding herself of the way the picture is supposed to be when everything is laid out. "This is about friends. Jim, Mark, Chris, Birck, and Howland. My friends."

The crown of her head is just by my knee. "That's it," I say, reaching over and touching her. "No physique critique. No discussions of income. I think we're getting somewhere." My immediate visions are a little spongy, however. I see us, Kirby and Neilanne, wearing heavy, dark dresses and serving unspiked punch to a stream of fit young men. I see myself shaking five strong hands, hands that smell like mixed nuts or brownies. I see the whole household friendly, brotherly, the kind of place where everyone washes their pajamas and underwear together. I know this will be good for Neilanne—she needs to get beyond things—but I think I will prefer our Saturdays at the Craft Center.

"It's the way I see my future," Nongqause says.

I tell her that I really have to be getting along because I have a class at 3:30, but how does dinner on Tuesday sound? I'll bake some bread or make a vegetable casserole, whatever she'd like. Nongqause is smiling, agreeable; she rubs her slightly round stomach with a large hand.

"Let's do it, Kirby," she says. "A light meal. Just you and me."

"Low cal, high fiber—that's us," I say.

"Right." But out of the corner of my eye I think I see Nongqause, or is it Neilanne, frown and pull anxiously at the fringe of her blue silk scarf. She is always considering something, I tell myself, something that seems very important, and I should not worry. Like the rest of us she's perplexed because she can't figure it all out.

That is not a flaw, of course. That is the best of it.

She waves to me through the screen door as I pull out of the dirt driveway. I wave back. We will see each other later, when we are in the same state of mind.

During the drive to the community college where I'll teach a class on Virginia Woolf, I allow myself a pat on the back. Neilanne has been launched, and no matter what happens, it probably wouldn't have started the way it did without me. Brag a little, I tell myself. She's much better off than you were six months after you kicked Larry out. She's benefited from your mistakes.

Marie, of course, would disagree.

"You're a teacher, not a guru," she told me once when she saw me weeding my herb garden. "And more than that," she says, "you're just one woman."

"So?" Marie is still married. I want to respect that.

"So don't lead this Neilanne, this student of yours, off on your goose chase."

"I'm just lending her some books," I say, offering Marie a handful of basil leaves. "And listening to her."

Marie shakes her head. "I know you, Kirby. You're good-hearted and lonely as hell. You let that girl make her own bed."

"She's young."

"She'll follow you too far."

"Hey," I say, loosening the soil around the thyme, "I didn't get her into those clothes or those spiritual things. Just a few books. Basic stuff. Like what you gave me for Christmas."

Marie has two children—a boy and a girl—but, ultimately, she understands. "Just leave her some room, Kirby. She looks so . . . so . . . ."

"We all get confused," I say.

I have to admit that Marie scores some points. I have my

weaknesses, my hopes for good minds and good hearts. When Neilanne enrolled in my Basic Composition class, it was rescue at first sight. This tall, lanky woman with too much eye liner and red, shiny boots. The only student I'd ever had who pulled out a compact while I was still arranging the discussion groups. I knew the minute I saw her that Neilanne Larrieu would heat up to a perfect boil before the term was over. Something in her face and the possessive way she held her brand new story anthology sent a signal. At the time, I couldn't really put my finger on it, on her attraction, although now after countless afternoons on her rug or in my back yard, I think I've defined what I need to. My mother always said that you could tell a girl who'd "done it" by the look on her face—the shadow of the blemish of knowledge, I guess. Well, it's not quite like that. Neilanne's not blemished. But she was definitely in the shadows, right behind the curtain and ready to burst through when I first met her. As I've told Marie a hundred times, I only happened to see the prescheduled train on the tracks. One way or another, Neilanne would have left Johnson Larrieu before summer ended.

Tuesday morning I decide to make some sesame bread, something Neilanne really likes. As I'm measuring the sesame seeds in a cup, I remember how she got that private name that hums in the back of my head, how I christened her. I first read it in a magazine when I was sunning on my stomach in the yard: Nongqause of the Xhosa, a prophet of change. But it didn't rise in my mind again until I saw Neilanne. She was complaining about Johnson, about how she'd really like to beat his butt just once. "To have him on his back and on the floor one time would do me months of good," she said. We were both up to our necks in red wine. "He can be such a wearing bastard."

Now Larry and I never came close to a knock down, drag out. Never even a half-hearted slap. It was all we could do to heat up a conversation, and I know I will always believe we were too easy on each other. But Nongqause. It came to me right then. Tall, silt black, thin as an evening bird's cry—the

African priestess would have the answer. *And those who wear trousers, whose pale legs shrivel in our Sun, shall be taken in a Whirlwind.*

Neilanne looked right at me when I named her. Then her eyes drifted above my head, toward the hand-plastered ceiling. She was spinning the stem of her wine glass between two fingers, spilling burgundy. "Just a joke," I said, "but a good one. It's got a real point."

"Nong-qa-oos-eh." She spoke slowly.

"A prophet from somewhere in Africa. A woman. She had a clean way of getting rid of white men." I smiled, looking at her stained napkin. "With whirlwinds."

"But I don't want to get rid of white men or any men," she said, taking a deep breath. "Just Johnson. He's the bad case."

That, of course, is what Neilanne thought she thought. She didn't completely understand herself—the real rock bottom of her anger—until a few weeks later. We're always needing whirlwinds, I tell myself as I begin to sift flour and soda. Something to suck the mistaken hope right out of us. Johnson Larrieu found himself spinning in a serious storm when he tried to slip through Neilanne's door that last time. She let him have it. Sent him back to his Buick with his tail tucked, she said. From then on it's been brand new things only—cotton clothes, vegetarian entrees, Joni Mitchell on the stereo I lent her. And me.

While the bread's in the oven I decide to pick over my garden so I can offer Neilanne anything extra that I might have. Unfortunately, there's not much—it's still too early in the season—but there are a few flowers along the fence, pansies mostly. A bouquet will do fine since as far as I'm concerned Neilanne and I always have something to celebrate. Every day. We are women who know where we are going, and we are happy about it. It doesn't take a crystal ball to see that.

I change my clothes and wrap the pansy stems in a wet napkin and tin foil while the bread cools. Nongqause, I think, will look absolutely elegant and forbidding with a blossom or two in her hair. Cool, beautiful, strong with a voice that is about to speak. Her skin will burnish and bronze as the sun sets behind the farmhouse. We will drink wine in the stretching shade. And next door, next door those young men will hear us and the best hints of our laughter. They will smell the odors of our meal as they stand in their cold, white pantry separating laundry.

And while they listen, we will practice fortune telling, making it—card by card, face by face, move by move—into our own little art.

When I get to the farm, I do all I can to keep my madras skirt out of the briar bushes that lead to the back door. The sesame bread is still very warm, absolutely pleading for the unsalted butter Neilanne has in her refrigerator. As I knock on the doorframe, I see pansy blossoms on my baggy blouse and in the crook of my elbow. Neilanne will love this; I am overloaded and falling apart at her doorstep.

No answer. I knock again, tapping above the audible back-beat of a jazz tune I don't recognize. Neilanne dosn't usually play music that can be heard outside, so I think she must be excited, souped up, ready to test some funny idea. That's great, that's wonderful. It's about time she stopped being so self-contained.

And then she is there, her black hair down to her shoulders—loose, wavy, the sheen of twilight near her eyes. She's in a pink bathrobe, on the other side of the screen.

"I should have called you," she whispers, bending toward me.

"Am I too early?" I ask, shifting the bread to my other arm. "Are you sick?"

Neilanne looks over her shoulder, down the hallway. "No," she says, pulling at a large, dangling earring that used to be mine. "I wanted to call."

"Why?" I hold the flowers where she can see them. I tilt them toward her.

"It's Jim," she says, bending lower, her lips brushing the rusty screen. "Jim's here."

"Jim."

Neilanne tightens the belt on her robe. Through the drooping silhouettes of the pansies I can see that her feet are bare. "It's a long story."

No. I shake my head. No, no. It's the easiest story in the

world. I look at her, never wavering, not moving. The bread I have baked is the temperature of my body now, just as warm, just as firm. The flowers nod over the knuckles of my hand.

"You could still let me in," I say, seeing how she is pale with bath powder as she moves back from the door, her lips parted like wet fingers. "You could still open this thing, you know."